E

D1710940

By the same author:

THE CUTTING EDGE

AN INNER SANCTUM MYSTERY

THE
STICKING
POINT

KEN JACKSON

SIMON AND SCHUSTER

NEW YORK

First Printing

SBN 671-20884-5
Library of Congress Catalog Card Number: 79-139633
Designed by Jack Jaget
Manufactured in the United States of America
By The Book Press Inc., Brattleboro, Vt.

THE STICKING POINT

ONE

He crouched in the way country people call hunkered down, his heels apart and planted solidly into the yielding ground, his buttocks suspended inches above it. His arms, loose across his thighs, cradled a pump twelve-gauge shotgun, a Winchester model 97, its ancient, full-choke barrel dusted silver from more than fifty years of wear. He had put six duck loads, number 4 shot, into the gun, one in the barrel ready to fire. He would need one or, at the most, two of the shells, but he liked the assurance of margin. His thumb lay across the gun's jutting hammer, occasionally testing its tension.

The sun, soon to be down behind hills to the west, sent hazed light through the thick leaves of the elm tree whose trunk hid him from the backyard of the house he watched, dappling the dark-brown ground. He had squatted there for almost an hour.

He kept patience, not tired and never considering discouragement. He had often sat the same way, waiting for squirrels to accept silence as safety and show themselves to rifle death or for a deer to walk unsuspectingly to a stand he'd held for five hours. He had smoked two cigarettes during his wait; now he lighted another, blew out smoke in a high-velocity stream that disappeared in the steady breeze.

He prided himself on being careful and sure—almost everything he had done all his life proved that.

He knew that on a cool, September summer evening a man who owned a home with a farm behind it would walk out into his back yard to look at his land, to smell the air and scan the sky. He waited for his man to come.

He gave no emotional evaluation to what he would do; he had been born without the ability to do so. Carefully, he had made his intellectual distinction; he had calculated the chance that he would be caught and found it almost nonexistent.

To him, then, his act would be not only permissible but desirable, for, underneath the thin layer of his pleasant personality, lay the cruel, unthinking violence of a wolf. It pleased him to be able to satisfy it.

He decided as he waited that he liked this better than deer or squirrel hunting; this carried keener implication, implacable surety, a necessary duty to himself not to fail and to do nothing wrong. If a deer escaped, there would always be another deer and another chance. If a man escaped, he might never flush into the open again.

He pulled the hammer of his gun to half cock, listened to the muted but menacing click, thought back over the controllable factors that too few people thought of or were able to control.

He had stolen a pickup truck that morning, parked it on a gravel road two hundred yards through the thick woods at his back. Anyone who saw it would think it belonged to a squirrel hunter, and if anyone, by any chance, marked it, he would be marking a truck that would be abandoned before the night ended, fifty miles away. Shotguns are hard, if not impossible, to trace, and his would be on the lake bottom after it had done its job. Antique or not, it was a deadly, completely reliable gun. He knew his shells were fresh; he had fired five from the same box through the same gun that morning. He knew the long-barreled pattern. He could blast a four-inch hole through inch-thick board at ten yards, and he intended to close the range to less than that.

He knew Alexander was at home; his car was parked in the drive, and a radio or phonograph played inside the house.

A woman opened the back door of the house and walked out to the patio. He cupped his cigarette and tensed. Alexander wasn't married. He hadn't expected a woman. She wore tight, white shorts and a yellow knitted halter, had long, dark-red hair, and seemed to be about twenty.

A new excitement began to grow in him. He did not alter his basic intent.

"Come on out, Ben," she said through the screen door. "We could play football in this yard."

Alexander, carrying two glasses, pushed open the door with his shoulder. "We'll sit on the patio awhile," he said. "I like this time of evening best of all."

They walked a few steps toward his tree, sat in canvas lounge chairs. Alexander passed one of the glasses to her.

"It's so quiet and so peaceful here," she said.

"That's why I like living out of town," Alexander said. "You're going to like it, too."

He put out his cigarette against the tree, pulled the hammer to full cock, and stood up slowly, cramped a little from the long wait, but feeling himself move as he wanted

9

to, smoothly and purposefully, like a cat covering the last few feet between it and a bird. He felt isolated and all-powerful. He took five steps before Alexander saw him, and the range had shortened to seven or eight yards, exactly right. "All right, Ben," he said. "I told you. Now." "No. Jesus, no . . ." Alexander said.

He shot him in the belly, not needing to aim but shooting halfway up from his hip as he had hundreds of times on quail covey rises. The heavy shot smashed Alexander, who had tried to stand, over the side of the chair and to the patio slab. He probably died before he hit. His glass broke on the concrete, and liquid and ice scattered.

The girl had frozen in motion with her glass part way to her mouth. She looked at him, not at Alexander's body, and he pumped his gun as he swung it toward her. He didn't shoot her. His excitement had swelled to a new, claiming need. While she stared at him in shock, her eyes uncomprehending, he put the gun down on the concrete, walked to her, lifted her out of the chair with his left hand, and with his right, tore the halter from her body. He clutched a full breast in each hand, began to push her back down, and she whimpered thinly. He lost control when he heard her, hit her viciously in the side of the head with his fist and let her fall to the concrete, stunned. He jerked at the waistband of her shorts, ripped them loose and down and off. When she was naked, he pushed her onto her back, took down his pants and shorts and raped her in driving, unrelenting violence.

He stood, made himself neat, got his gun and, while she cried hysterically, brokenly, into her hands, shot her in the head at a range of three feet. To make absolutely certain, he shot Alexander in the head. The compacted charges destroyed the shapes of their skulls, mashed them.

He stood still a moment, measuring two kinds of satisfaction and satiety. He smiled, turned quickly and walked past his stalking tree and into the woods. He went steadily, not hurrying. He came out of the woods and onto the shoulder of the road at the exact place he had parked the pickup, climbed into it, started it and drove away.

TWO

〰〰〰〰〰〰〰

When I answered the phone in my apartment, the secretary said, "Just a second, please, Mr. Blade, for Mr. Norman," and Curt came on the line in almost that short a time.

"You had a long-distance call here at the magazine about five minutes ago, Jud," Curt said. "From Kit Marlow in Catherton, Oklahoma."

"Did he leave his number?"

"No, just his name."

"Thanks, Curt."

"That's where you went in June," Curt said. "Who's Kit Marlow?"

I give only two persons answers about my trips and what I do on them, and Curt is one of the two. "Kit's the sheriff there," I said.

"You told me when you got back that everything was all right, that you were clear of any involvement," Curt said.

"Everything was all right." It was for me, but five

people had died violently. I had killed the one who most deserved to die, indirectly, but I had killed him.

"Why would the sheriff call you?"

"I'll have to get off the phone and call him back to find out," I said.

"I'm not trying to pry, Jud," he said.

"I know, Curt. Thank you for the message."

"You're welcome."

"I'll call you if it's anything important and I'll see you."

I hung up. It would be a waste of time and imagination to wonder about Kit's call, so I picked up the phone without taking my hand from it and placed a call to him in Catherton.

While the operator did her work, I looked out at the gloom of September drizzle on Chicago's Near North and remembered the flat Oklahoma sun and the tree leaves that had never had soot on them; the Catherton operator's half-nasal, half-southern accent sounded particularly good to me. "Sure, honey, you don't need a number," she told my girl in Chicago. "Sheriff's not at his office, he's prob'ly over to Ma Maxwell's for coffee. That time of day." She found Kit at Ma Maxwell's, wherever and whatever that was.

"Jud," he said. "You got back to me in good hurry."

"Sure," I said. "What is it, Kit?"

"You Yankees always got to bust right in on things. How you been?"

"Fine."

"Plenty magazine stories?"

I had gone to Catherton in June with the cover story that I was a writer for *Now* magazine. I don't work on *Now*. Curt and I own it. "Always plenty of those, Kit; what is it?"

"Done any fishin'?"

"Been out to the ball park a few times."

I had stayed in Oklahoma long enough that I should have learned you don't hurry Oklahomans; they happen to you when they're ready; the President should learn to use them at diplomatic tables.

"Cubs been goin' good," Kit said.

"Think they'll hold up?"

"They weak on pitchin'." He waited four or five seconds. "You hear what happened here day 'fore yestiddy?"

"No, Kit." I said.

"Figgered it would be all over the country. You remember Ben Alexander, don't you?"

"Sure." Alexander was the county attorney in Catherton; young, nervous, eager, not long in his office. He and Kit and Swimmer Early and I had worked together in June.

"Some son of a bitch shot Ben," Kit said.

"Kill him?"

"Shot 'im twice with a twelve gauge and heavy loads at real short range," Kit said. "In the belly and in the head." He didn't confirm death but he didn't need to; I know what a shotgun does at close range. "Killed Ben's girl friend, too. Beth Nichols. Ben was fixin' to marry 'er. Don't think you got to meet 'er when you was down here, Jud, but she was a real nice, real pretty girl. He raped 'er 'fore he killed 'er." He said it matter of factly, but he wouldn't have called me if he felt that way about it and he wouldn't have called to tell me he had caught the man who had done it; Kit didn't hunt publicity.

"You have ideas about who did it?" I asked.

"Got ten or twelve," he said. "Haven't been able to git nowhere with none of 'em."

"Wonder if I could help." I asked.

"You did last time," he said, "but I wouldn't want to put you out none."

14

"I can get the magazine to assign me to the story," I said.

"I was bettin' you could," Kit said.

Kit knew that I was something other than a magazine writer, knew that I had once been with the FBI, but he had never pressed me to know more and he wouldn't now. This was Tuesday afternoon. "I'll be there Thursday morning," I said.

"Be proud to have you. I'll git you a place to stay."

"See you then, Kit."

"See you, Jud. Lookin' forward to it."

We both hung up. I got a beer, a Dortmunder, from the refrigerator and opened it. I don't like to catalog or even remember most of my past, but my mind does it automatically; I suppose everyone's mind does. This would be my twenty-first trip in the more than twelve years since two men had raped my wife, Maurie, on the floor of our bedroom after one had held my service gun to my head while the other tied me to our bed. When they had finished with my lovely Maurie, one of them cut her throat. They left me to remember it.

I've never quit hunting the two and I've never found them. I still pray that sometime I will. Maurie left me more money than I will ever need and half of *Now* magazine. Curt, her brother, runs it. I have one thing to do with my life and the abilities I have: I hunt, find and sometimes execute rapist–killers, anywhere and anytime.

I don't have any legal right—I left the FBI after Maurie died—but I claim the blood right. In twenty trips, I've failed twice. Of the eighteen I've caught or have helped others catch, fifteen are dead, one way or another, and the other three are in prison. I hope they rot there.

This would be the first time I had gone to a place the second time.

I picked up the phone and called Pat at her art gallery. Pat is the second person I tell about my trips; she did most of the putting-me-together after Maurie died and she and I love each other in a special, needing and fulfilling way.

"Hi," I said.

"Hello today, love."

"I have to leave in the morning," I said.

"Then we'll have a long dinner and a long night," she said.

"They're always short."

"Too short. Where, Jud?"

"I'm going back to Oklahoma. Kit called me; I told you about him."

"I thought you had some kind of a rule about going to the same place twice," she said.

"No. It hasn't ever come up before."

"We've had a good summer."

"And we'll have a good fall," I said. I like fall better than the other seasons, all of it; the late-night and the early-morning fogs, the rains that are still not tinged deeply with winter's thin bitterness, the pale yellows and the bittersweets, the pervasive wood smoke that drifts nostalgia of known and unknown memories. "We can go to Gus's or over to the Red Star."

Pat knew what I wanted to hear and said it: "I'd rather cook for us and spend the evening at home."

"What time?"

"Seven?"

"Fine. I'll see you then, baby."

"I like to hear you call me baby. It's because I'm so big."

She is five-ten and about a hundred and fifty, long, dark-red hair, sky-blue eyes that can soften and darken to violet for me. I like everything about her, including her size. I told her so before we hung up.

I packed a bag, mostly with slacks and sport shirts; they aren't formal in Oklahoma, especially around the sheriff's office. I got out my gun and checked it and the spring clip that holds it in the side pocket of my pants and throws it into my hand when I need it thrown there in a hurry. It's a flat, very light .32 with a barrel an inch longer than usual. A lot of people, some of whom should know, say a .32 doesn't carry enough impact, enough shock power, to stop a determined, powerful man. They're wrong; if you hit a man in the center of the chest, a .32 stops him, no matter how determined and powerful he is, and when I shoot at a man, I hit him where I intend to hit him.

My throwing knife, six and half inches of blade and balance, slipped smoothly from its thin sheath. When I'm working, I fasten it between and above my shoulder blades. I whipped it with my forearm and wrist at a dart board I keep fastened to my combination living room–den wall. It turned twice in the fourteen feet or so and thudded into the board, not more than an inch off center. I pulled it loose and put it back in the sheath, packed it and the gun with my clothes.

I called the garage and Pete said they'd have my car, a 1963 Corvette that has been tooled to take anything I'm liable to meet on any road, ready in the morning.

I was ready to travel, eager to. Almost three months of relative inactivity are too much for me. I called Curt and asked him to meet me at the club, put on a raincoat against the drizzle and caught a cab at the LaSalle corner. I needed an hour of good, fast handball. I'm six-three and two-twenty and I don't intend to let my weight get any higher than that. I also intend to keep my reflexes, and handball sharpens them better than any game I know.

Curt was waiting. "What was the call?" he asked.

"Kit needs a little help," I said. "Let's play before we talk about it."

"Are you going?"

"Tomorrow, Curt."

He served without saying anything more. Curt doesn't approve of what I do although he tries hard to understand why I have to do it. We're matched about evenly at handball, but he spent too much time thinking whether or not he should try to talk me out of the trip, and I beat him four out of four games. We showered, dressed and went to the bar, sat at a small table in the corner.

"What kind of help does a sheriff need?" he asked after a waiter had brought bourbon for me and scotch for him.

"You have to think when you play handball or you get outmaneuvered and beat four out of four times," I said.

He grinned at me. "Dammit, Jud, you know I worry."

"And when you get beat, you have to sign for the drinks," I said.

"All right. I'm not going to try to talk you out of it, but how can you help a sheriff in Oklahoma? What does he need help with?"

"A rape and a double murder, Curt. And I don't know how I can help him, but he's a friend and I'll try."

"At least this time you'll be with the law, on its side."

"At least," I said. I wasn't sure of this. Kit had the help he needed on the law's side. He might need someone with more freedom and less scruples.

"Do you need anything?" Curt asked. "I set up a place for you to stay the last time you went to Oklahoma."

"Kit said he'd take care of that," I said.

"Laura and I have a dinner, so I've got to go now," he said. "What do you expect me to say to you before I do?"

" 'Be careful.' "

"That's it. I'm glad you're thinking of it. Hurry back, Jud."

"Soon as I can, Curt."

18

Pat had waited for me to light the fire she had laid, a rite we both like to celebrate, and we watched the birchbark burn blue and gold-red before the logs caught. "A four-log fire," I said. "An occasion."

"You rate four logs," she said. We sat on her outsized couch, not touching but close enough to touch and hold when we wanted to, which we would—and later did. "So many goodbyes, and always this way," she said at two in the morning.

"Would you want another way?"

She turned to me, in the bed, the warmth of her velvet and welcome. "There isn't any other way."

We had been together seven hours and she hadn't asked me about the trip. She never does until I talk about it. I appreciate the rarity of her.

"I told you about Kit," I said. "Did I talk about Ben Alexander?"

"No, love."

"Ben was the county attorney in Catherton."

"Was?"

"Someone killed him and his fiancée. He also raped her."

"Did you know her?"

"No," I said. "I knew Ben."

She pushed her head into the hollow of my shoulder she claims as hers. "Do you know what you'll do when you get there?"

"No. First, I'll see Kit."

"Jud, do you ever know what you'll do when you start on a trip?"

"I know the one thing I intend to do. I don't know how I'll go about it."

"Hurry back to me," she said.

"I will, baby."

"Call me baby again."

"Baby. You're my baby."

"You're mine. I'm going to have to prove it again."

"We'll both prove it."

"Oh, yes, love, it takes both of us."

THREE

Oklahoma and Catherton looked sun-tired in the late, bright September morning, as if it had been a blazing summer and the trees and grass would be glad when they could give up completely for the year. Fall hadn't gotten here yet. I parked in front of the City–County building where Kit had his office, got out and stretched away the hundred and fifty miles from Springfield, Missouri, where I had spent the night. The Corvette and I had taken the trip easily.

When I had left in June, two Indian prisoners had been working on the courthouse lawn across the street from the City–County building, or, to be exact, one had been mowing slowly while the other watched. I half expected to see the same two now, because, at their pace, the job would never have been done, but no one was working. The yellowing lawn didn't need it. I went up the short walk and into the building.

"Mornin', Blade," the tall, stringy man behind the

counter said. "You some behind time." He had a leathered, hawk's face, spare and timelessly old.

"I slept extra," I said. "It's Fred Peters, isn't it?"

"Ain't changed since you was here last. Kit said you'd be comin' in, told me to look for you." Peters was Kit's undersheriff. "You drink it black, don't you?"

"Black's fine, Fred."

He poured coffee for me from an electric pot into a thick, white mug, set it on the counter. "You know," he said, "after you left here, I read that magazine *Now* for two, three weeks. Never did see nothin' about us in there."

"They don't use half of what I write," I said.

"Same way here," he said. "Kit don't do half what I tell 'im to do. You down here because of Ben?"

"That's how come they sent me." People in Oklahoma seldom say "why." It's "how come." I didn't know whether or not Peters knew Kit had called me and I decided to stay with the *Now* cover story.

"Take a real son of a bitch to do what that son of a bitch did to Ben and Beth," Fred said.

"Has Kit arrested anyone?"

He leaned back in his chair and propped his brown cowboy boots on his steel desk and didn't seem to hear me. "Trouble is, this county's so full of sons of bitches a man can't tell 'em apart without he's got a program, and ain't nobody never printed a program."

"Where is Kit?"

"Comin' in the door behind you."

Kit did. I put my coffee cup down and turned to meet him. He wore the only uniform I had ever seen him wear —starched khakis, faded to near white, shined, black cowboy boots, no hat and no gun. He is slight and corded but strong, not fragile, as sun dark as a full-blood Indian; he is a quarter Cherokee. His hair, cut short, and his

22

eyebrows, grown long, are heavy and silver white, and they emphasize the unfaded blue of his eyes. He looked tired, and I could imagine the hours he had put in since Sunday. "I'm real glad you could come, Jud," he said as he put out his hand.

Shaking hands with him was like shaking hands with a warm and vibrant board. "Real glad to be here," I said. He poured a cup of coffee. "How many more calls?" he asked Peters.

"Four, five," Peters said.

"All the same thing?"

" 'Bout the same. Two was people wantin' to know how come you ain't caught anybody. Two was people know who done it but they ain't gonna tell nobody but you and will call back. Other'n was old Sam Basket, and he said he sure as hell ain't gonna vote for you next election," Peters said.

"Sam ain't never voted for me," Kit said. "Come on in, Jud."

We went through the first door on the right side of the hall and into his office. It looked the same as it had when I left it—a metal desk with a scarred top, a leather-covered sofa along one wall, three brown-painted straight chairs. Kit sat in the padded chair behind his desk. "Pull you up a chair," he said.

I did. "When was the last time you got any sleep?" I asked him.

"Tuesday night," he said. "Shouldn't've gone to bed then, neither. Jud, I am up a tall tree and every way I turn on my limb there's a new hound dawg rarin' up on the trunk and bayin' hard at me."

"Sounds tough, Kit," I said.

He opened the shallow middle drawer of his desk and took out three red, exploded shotgun shells and three cigarette butts in small, plastic bags and a sheaf of eight-by-ten glossy photographs. He pushed the pictures across his desk to me. The top one showed an overall view of a concrete patio with a man's and a woman's bodies crumpled on it. There were two aluminum and plastic chairs, two canvas lounge chairs, one of them tipped onto its side, a small metal table. A broken glass lay beside the man's body, another beside the woman's. The woman's body was naked except for canvas shoes; there were two small bundles of cloth near it. Even in black and white, the picture was very graphic and very messy. I could tell that the man and woman had once had heads, but no one could tell what those heads had looked like.

"Frank Butler, my deputy—you met him—took those Monday," Kit said. "Climbed clear up on top of Ben's house to git that one."

"Who found them, Kit?"

"Me. Ben was supposed to be in court first thing Monday mornin', and Bessie couldn't git 'im on the phone when he didn't show up. Beth didn't have any folks around here to worry about 'er. I went out to see about Ben when Bessie called me, and you lookin' at what I seen when I got there." Kit's accent deepened in stress; it sounded strong now. I leafed through the rest of the pictures. The close-ups were messier. Shot had cut Alexander nearly in two.

"What about the shells and the cigarette butts?"

"That's all we found. He shot Beth once, Ben twice. He made damn sure."

"The butts or the shells mean anything to you or the lab boys from the state? They are in on it, aren't they?"

"Been thicker'n fleas on a lazy 'possum. Up here and went through Ben's safe 'fore I got around to it. But you know I can buy two hunderd boxes of shells like that 'fore noon today and I can git them cigarettes in any drugstore or café or grocery store in town."

"Or in any town."

"Now you climbin' up the tree with me. I can tell you how he did it and what he did it with, a twelve-gauge shotgun. I can tell you he waited three cigarettes' worth before he done it, and I can show you the tree he waited behind so's he could git it done." He took the shells out of their sack and waved one back and forth under his nose. "Hell, I can even smell the powder that done it. I can tell you reasons why somebody done it." He put down the shell, ranged the three in an orderly row before him, and leaned back in his chair. "But I can't tell you who. I ought to be able to. I, by God, ought to. A man who knows his county and the people in it—and I damn sure thought I did—ought to be able to tell you who, but I can't, Jud."

I gave the pictures back to him. He put them, the shells and the cigarette butts back into the drawer. He leaned over and opened the bottom-left drawer of his desk, raised up with an unlabeled pint bottle, uncapped it. "What was it the governor of North Carolina said to the governor of South Carolina?" he said.

"He said, 'It has been a long, long time between drinks.' "

"You up on your history," he said. He handed me the bottle. I am never going to like moonshine, even if it has, as Kit says his has, been aged in a charred oak keg for several years, with the keg tied in the top of a pine tree to let the wind rock it, but, for sudden, surprising stomach heat that spreads all the way to your feet, you can't beat it. Or tie it.

"Shooo," I said when I lowered the bottle.

"You at least learned to speak you some Cherokee while

you was down here," he said. He took his drink, longer than mine, capped the bottle and put it back in its drawer. "All right, what does it look like to you, Jud?"

"Kit, I don't know enough about it for it to look like anything."

"You know about as much as me. You never did see Ben's place, did you?"

"No." The only place I had seen Ben had been in his courthouse office, then only twice.

"He lived two miles outta town, out east. Bought a half section out there not too long back. Run some cattle. Lived out there by hisself. Now whoever done it knew the place, went out there intendin' to do it and had planned it all out. He waited behind a big old elm tree in Ben's back yard, waited quite a spell, long enough to smoke three cigarettes, anyhow, until Ben and Beth come out into the yard, then killed 'em. Stands to reason he shot Ben first, raped Beth, then shot 'er. He could've been five hunderd miles from here before anybody knew it had been done."

"Do you think he was?"

"Prob'ly not. Prob'ly not more'n ten or twenty, if that far."

"Then you think someone from around here did it," I said.

"I got to think that." He said it doggedly, a little defensively, which wasn't like Kit, not at all. I sensed that he held back.

"Why, Kit?"

"Ben had enemies in this county, more enemies than anybody, even me. You got to understand these people, Jud, and it is hard to understand 'em without you live your life here. I arrest 'em, they expect it, because it's what I have to do, and it's between them and me, private like. But they figger Ben filed the charge against 'em in the first place, or against their kin, which is about the same thing, figger he had the choice whether or not to do it, and Ben was awful eager and hled more'n anybody ever did before in this county. Then he was the one got up in court and prosecuted, made 'em look bad in front of a whole courtroom full of folks, sent 'em off to the pen. They take what Ben had to do and did personal, real personal."

"And someone would kill him for that, for doing his job?"

Kit looked at me with the patient understanding of a fourth-grade teacher, but, when he talked, it sounded as if he was trying to convince himself as much as he was trying to explain to me. "I can offhand name you twenty or thirty," he said. "When folks down here take somethin' personal, they do somethin' about it."

I got up from my chair and walked to the three windows along the wall behind his desk, looked out at the square, three-storied courthouse and its lawn. It looked sleepy. Kit came to stand next to me. An Indian woman, carrying a baby, with two small, coal-haired youngsters following her, went slowly up the walk and into the building.

"Sara Goodknife," Kit said. "Goin' in to talk to the welfare people again. Her husband run off and I ain't been able to locate 'im. He'll be back; they run off but they don't stay. This is home."

"It's hard for me to understand these people, the way you say they are. I don't doubt you, Kit, not for a second, but it's hard." You don't doubt someone's word in Oklahoma or even talk carelessly enough to imply doubt. I had found that out in June.

"Sure it is," Kit said. "Like I say, you got to live your life here."

Kit knew his county and its people and he had never talked idly to me, but I could see a piece of an old pattern

27

here, or thought I might see it. "All right if I pry?" I asked.

"You pry ahead. I asked you down here."

"How much crime do you have in this county, Kit?"

"More'n some. You saw the knives come out when you was down here before. It's a poor county and when you got poor people, you got people who will now and then break open a cabin door and take whatever they can find. You got people, mostly professionals from outside, who will steal cattle; it's a big county with a lot of cattle scattered over a lot of hills and in a lot of trees, so they are easy to steal. You got people who are sometimes desperate enough or mean enough to take a gun and go after what they want. And, like I said, you got people who will fight you or kill you out of personal pride, good people who will do it. I guess we got more'n our share, Jud." He waited for me to ask something more and I hunted for the right way to ask it.

"Not that kind of crime, Kit. I'm talking about the only profitable kind, the organized kind. The lake makes this a resort area. You've got poor people, but you've got a lot of rich people who come here, like the ones out at the Pinnacle Club." I had stayed at the club in June. It had a hundred members and I doubt that any of the hundred was worth much less than a million dollars. "You've got a lot of tourists with traveling money in their pockets. I'm talking about the gambling, the women, maybe drugs."

He looked at me levelly, turned and went back to his chair and sat. I went back to mine across the desk from him. "I knew this'd come up," he said. "We got some just lately, the last year or so. North end of the county is open. They police themselves, so it's orderly for the most part, but it's wide open. I ain't stopped it."

"Could you have stopped it if Ben gave you the warrants and backed you all the way?"

Kit had known me less than four months and had been with me in all for only a week. His admission that he hadn't been able to stop something in his county had come hard for him. Now he saw or sensed what I was leading up to, and that seemed to come harder. "I asked you down here to help me," he said, "so I am not about to beat around any bush with you. I ain't takin'. I ain't never took."

"But Ben did." If it was hard for him to say, I'd say it for him.

"Ben did, the last seven, eight months or so," Kit said.

"You know or are you guessing?" I asked.

"No guessin'. Would never say it if I was guessin'. I liked Ben, Jud. Liked 'im a lot."

"How do you know he was taking?" I asked.

"I asked 'im."

"And he told you?"

"Ben couldn't lie to me, Jud. State boys started crackin' down on the places up north on the lake nine months ago. First coupla raids, they dragged back a truckload of booze after they planted somebody to buy a drink across the bar, which is illegal here. Boys up there was hurt, bad, in the pocket, so they come to me first. I told 'em no. Them and me and Ben had had a kind of gentlemen's agreement, only maybe that ain't the right term, because I ain't no way sure I'm a gentleman and I know damn well most of them ain't. I let 'em sell booze as long as they run tight and right; resort area'd die off if I didn't. After I told 'em no, they went straight outta here and across to the courthouse, to Ben. Next time the state boys raided up there, they didn't git enough booze to git a bluejay drunk —and ever' time after that, too. They quit."

"Ben tipped the people up there in advance," I said.

"For a fact," Kit said. He filled a bulldog black pipe from a Pliofilm pouch, lighted it. "State boys got to come th'ough the county sheriff and the county attorney; it's the law. Only Ben and me knowed. Since it wasn't me, it had to be Ben, so I asked 'im."

"And he told you?"

"Ben was young and eager, Jud; he was also hungry—and, in a way, they forced it on 'im. He told me they told 'im he either took so's he'd be a guarantee for 'em, or he got beat next votin', and Ben didn't want to git beat. He didn't even have to ask for it or go after it. They brung it to 'im in cash, first of the month, just like a regular paycheck. He bought that place and he wanted to marry Beth and he needed more'n a county attorney's wages, so he took. I ain't defendin', but I'm not condemnin', neither. I don't know many would've turned it down."

"You did, Kit."

"I'm different. I don't want nothin'. I am too old to worry about gittin' beat in a election. I am too ornery and stubborn to threaten. And I never really got tested except the once; when they had Ben, they didn't need me."

"Did Ben get greedy?" I asked. It's easy for someone in Ben's place—the place he had held—to get greedy. It is not a sensible thing to do.

"I don't know. I'd say he prob'ly didn't, but that's a guess."

"Did he decide he wanted out?"

"I don't know," Kit said. "He had got used to that money. He owed more'n a little on the place."

"What about the state boys? Didn't they get suspicious?"

"Sure. They sent a fella named Don James up here near ever' week—he's up here now on the killin's—and he asked me a coupla thousand questions and he asked Ben a coupla thousand more. Him and Ben got to be

30

pretty close. Guess he gave up; anyhow he quit botherin us." He puffed hard on the pipe, grimaced, put it down on his desk top. "Smoked that damn thing so much my mouth feels like the inside of a rubber boot in the summertime."

"You didn't say anything to James about Ben?" I asked.

"Hell, a man couldn't do a thing like that." His voice and his look implied I was off base for asking. I reminded myself of what I know about the Oklahoma code.

"If Ben got greedy or if he wanted out, either one, Kit, the people up there could have killed him because it made good business sense to kill him," I said. "That gives us two streets to walk—the hate or revenge you've talked about, the personal kind, or good business, plain and simple. I believe I vote in favor of the business."

"I been goin' on the idea it's the hate or revenge," Kit said, "much as I hate to think somebody from around here done it. That's prob'ly because I'm out of my league on the other. It don't come easy to say it, but I am. That's how come I called you, Jud. You got down to it in a hurry. If you hadn't, I want you to know I would've brought it out into the open between us before too long."

"I know you would have." I wasn't ruling out Kit's concept of motive, but the circumstances made mine much more probable. "If it was business, Kit, it was probably a professional job, done by a professional killer, and whoever did it is probably more than five hundred miles away, spending his fee."

"I know that, Jud. And if it was, the chances of catchin' 'im are about the same as the chances of me gettin' called to Washington to replace old J. Edgar." He got up and began to walk back and forth in front of the windows, four or five steps up, the same distance back. "Now I don't know a lot about professional killers, but from what I hear

31

and read, it don't seem likely that one would mess up a killin' job by committin' rape."

Kit was wrong. Professional killers are, almost one hundred percent, psychopaths, and a psychopath will do anything if he is relatively sure he can get away with it. Killing, for them, doesn't involve emotion as most of us think of emotion; it doesn't affect the soul, because psychopaths don't have a soul or a concept of one; they were born without that; but killing can trigger strong sensual satisfaction in them and can excite and stimulate a hunger for further sensual satisfaction, a lust for it. I hate to sound pedantic so I didn't explain that to Kit. "It's likely," I said. "How do you think I can help with this? By working under cover?"

"Hell, no. They ain't no such thing as under cover in this town or this county. Half or more of the people here already know about you from last time, and at least a quarter of 'em know you're back in town again, since you been here a good half hour."

This time he was right. I remembered the efficiency of the Oklahoma intelligence and information network. People knew who you were and what you were doing or were going to do long before you met them. "They know I'm a writer for *Now,* don't they?"

"You are, ain't you?" He grinned at me, his first grin since we had taken the drink.

"Sure I am," I said.

Peters opened the door without knocking and put his head and shoulders in. "James and Mercer out here," he told Kit.

"I told you about James," Kit said to me. "Mercer is his boss; he was up here once, just 'fore he pulled James off. They both been here since Monday and are likely to stay with it." He sat down. "Send 'em in," he told Peters. He didn't seem overly pleased to say it.

FOUR

ϒϒϒϒϒϒϒϒϒϒϒϒϒ

Kit went through introductions when the two men came into his office. We shook hands.

Haley Mercer was probably about my age, maybe two or three years older, but I hope time and circumstance have been easier on me, on the way I look. Bitterness and sardonic lack of patience laced his face. His short-clipped hair had grayed unevenly, almost in patches; it gave him a piebald look. He held his mouth to a thin, tight line. His small, black eyes covered me in a bleak, perfunctory inspection, glanced off to Kit, then to the window, off to the wall, where they lingered in rumination, back to me, and over to James to carry the message that I represented another cross to bear. He looked as if he made a habit of finding crosses.

Don James was in his middle thirties, easy and athletic and a contrast to Mercer. He wore the perpetually scrubbed, glowing clean look you sometimes see in a blond-haired person whose skin takes an almost translucent but deep, even tan, a look I envy. His gray-blue eyes leveled at me when we shook hands, surveyed me, showed they had made judgment, and welcomed me. He seemed directly pleasant but did not condescend to the sudden affability a lot of people affect when they meet a writer from *Now*, a writer who can spread names nationally for better or for worse.

Mercer clearly led the team, because he took over the conversation after both he and James had said hello. James didn't step back or away, but he assumed an expression of patient, understanding anonymity. "From *Now* magazine," Mercer said. "How about that? We have suddenly got important." He said it without sarcasm but with resignation and obvious unhappiness with necessary small talk. Amenities played no part in his life if he could help it.

"How often does a prosecuting attorney get killed?" I said.

"This is the first time in this state, in my state," Mercer said. "When we burn the man who did it, it ought to be the last time."

"How far have you gotten?" I asked him. I would try hard to like this man. I know how frustrating, how mind-bending a lawman's job can be. I know many—most—lawmen wear a shell through necessity, and, often, if you can penetrate the shell, you find a different person, a better one to know and to work with.

"How much have you told this man?" Mercer asked Kit.

"Not much," Kit said.

"There isn't much to tell," James said. "You can sum it up in one good paragraph. Motive from who knows how many people, a few clues that lead nowhere. Whoever did it did a clean job. A professional one."

"I showed Jud what I found," Kit said. "The shell

cases and the cigarette butts, the pictures Frank took." He sounded much more distant with Mercer and James than he did with me, not resentful of their intrusion into his territory, not spiteful over the fact that Mercer obviously considered himself in charge, just distant. Sheriffs and state bureau men are not always overly cooperative with each other. Sheriffs know that state men are appointed, part of the patronage system, and they are suspicious of them; they know that state men are here today and gone the day after tomorrow, not answerable to local critics and voters. On the other hand, state men know that sheriffs are elected largely on personality and are not always capable or qualified, so the suspicion is mutual.

"We found footprints when we got here, Mr. Blade," James told me. "A hunting boot, crepe-soled, probably a nine and a half."

"Damn lucky to find them," Mercer said, "Marlow here let half the people in the county stomp around out there."

"I told you twice," Kit said evenly, "that there was folks in front of the house because I didn't have anybody to keep 'em shooed off, but nobody but me and my deputy went out in back. Anyway, half the people in this county wear huntin' boots half the time. Ben had a pair. He could'a made those tracks." He made it plain he didn't think the footprints meant much.

"All right, all right," Mercer said. "Maybe the prints will help and maybe not, but they're something. We've got so damn little." He sat on the corner of Kit's desk, picked up a copper letter opener and ran his thumb nervously up and down its edge.

"We've been back out to Ben's place this morning," James said. "Never hurts to give it one more try."

"Find anything?" Kit asked.

"No," Mercer said.

"Nothin' to find," Kit said.

Mercer reversed the letter opener and held it by the handle, pointed it at Kit. "Have you made that list we talked about?" he asked. "That list of men you think had reason to kill Alexander, the ones mean enough to do it?"

"In my head," Kit said.

"What the hell good does that do me?" Mercer asked. "We ought to be hauling in every one of them."

"Can't do a thing like that," Kit said. "Got to have a better reason. I'll write the list down for you, go over it with you, but I aim to take care of that end of it."

"You haven't," Mercer said.

I could feel tension build in the room. James could, too; he tried to lessen it. "Haley and I have got to get back to Oklahoma City," he said. "Pick up some clean clothes and check in at the Bureau."

Fred appeared in the open door. "Acre has come in again," he said to Kit.

"He drunk again?"

"Does a mule have a ass hole?"

"Take him back and put 'im to bed," Kit said. "Feed 'im this evenin', and he'll be sober enough to go on home."

"Don't you book drunks?" Mercer asked.

Kit picked up his cold pipe from the desk, prodded at the ashes with his forefinger, lighted a match deliberately, and drew until he got an even burn. "Now and then we book 'em," he said. "But old Acre is on 'is day off. He's got a wife and seven kids to home and he takes care of all of 'em without no help from the welfare. I book 'im, and he'll miss work tomorrow, pay a fine with money he needs to buy beans and gravy. He come in on his own account. He ain't caused no trouble, and as long as he's in here sleepin' it off, he won't cause none, so I figure he is welcome."

"Hell of a way to run things," Mercer said.

"Anybody asked you to shoot your mouth off?" Fred said. He came a step into the room.

Mercer looked at him blankly, as if he were wondering what he had said to touch Fred's temper. "I said it's a hell of a way to run things," he said. "No need to get your bowels in an uproar, old man."

"Old man, old man!" Fred screeched. "I was a lawman 'fore you was weaned. I'll be one, a workin' one, when you planted behind a desk in Oklahoma City kissin' political ass while yore own spreads."

"That's enough, Fred," Kit said.

Fred glared. He had balled his knotty old fists and had taken two steps toward Mercer. "Burns my ass," he said. "They come in here and try to take over, city big shots. Always tellin' and orderin'. Ain't got the manners of a he goat. You listen to me and listen hard, Mercer. I, by God, won't . . ."

"Take Acre on back, Fred, and put 'im to bed. Now," Kit said. "And would you please close the door on your way out."

Fred kept his old hawk's eyes on Mercer for three or four seconds, said nothing more, turned and pulled the door to behind him as he left.

"Old bastard is touchy," Mercer said. "Ought to be put out to pasture, Marlow."

"I am a little touchy myself," Kit said. He got out of his chair. "And gittin' more so. We had better git a couple things straight now, Mercer. This is my county, just like Fred is my undersheriff. You welcome here because it is your job to be here. I will be the first to say I prob'ly need you on these killin's, but the way I handle my people and my county business is my business. I flat aim for it to stay that way." He didn't raise his voice

37

when he spoke. He didn't sound belligerent or angry. He did sound as sure and as definite as a judge instructing a jury.

"We're all a little touchy, Kit," James said. "It's only natural. Everybody from the governor on down—maybe on up, too—is watching us, waiting for us to come up with something, crack the thing open. Haley and I both know we need to work with you to do it."

I wondered how many times a day he filled the role of diplomat. He did it well, without obvious intrusion and with good timing.

Mercer got up from the corner of Kit's desk and dropped the letter opener to its top. He grinned at Kit, but the expression only tightened the line of his lips, didn't reach to his eyes. "Don's right," he said. "And, like you say, Marlow, it's your county." He made no concession when he said it.

I felt the tension lessen a little as Kit sat down again, leaned over and knocked out his pipe into his metal wastebasket. I tried to ease it further.

"Did you find anything in Alexander's office safe when you opened it?" I asked Mercer and James. I made things worse.

"Who told you we opened it?" Mercer said.

"I told 'im," Kit said.

James jumped in again. "We found the usual, Mr. Blade," he said. "Maybe more of that than usual. Ben kept a lot of records, wrote a lot of personal notes to himself."

"But nothing that showed he had an idea of what was going to happen to him?" I asked.

"Nothing," James said. "We ought to get started, Haley. It's a long drive, and we need to get back here tonight."

"How come you told him, Marlow?" Mercer asked.

"No 'how come' to it," Kit said. "I was just bringin' Jud up to date on what has happened."

"I'm against letting the press in on investigations, any part of them," Mercer said. "They've got no right, and most of them show no responsibility. They're liable to spread confidential matter all over the country. Nothing personal, Blade. You've got your job, and we've got ours."

"Jud's a friend of mine and I treat 'im like a friend," Kit said. "It's no secret you had James open that safe, Mercer. Ever'body in Catherton knows it. Hell, come to think of it, it was in the *Tulsa World*. They even listed some of the stuff James found."

"All right, all right," Mercer said. "We aren't getting anywhere. You write down that list and we'll go over it in the morning."

"Told you I will," Kit said.

Mercer started for the door, his dismissal of the disagreements as blunt and sudden as his language.

"Glad to have met you, Mr. Blade," James said. He turned to follow Mercer.

"You, too," I said.

Mercer, with his hand on the doorknob, turned, and said to the room in general, "We'll get him. I intend for us to get him." He didn't say it to reassure himself and he didn't say it to heal the rift that had developed between him and Kit—which may, for all I knew, have been there before. He said it as a declaration, an affirmation of his faith in himself. He turned the knob, opened the door, and the two of them left.

Kit looked at the door after it had closed behind them. "Him and his boot prints," he said.

"He is on a tight string," I said. I didn't mean to excuse Mercer, but I tried to see reason for his erratic, irritating behavior.

39

Kit thought about it. "I don't like 'im much," he said. "Maybe some of it's my fault, though. He's doin' his job. He will git his butt burnt in the city, and when he gits back here, he'll want to haul in half the county for questionin'. These are my folks. I'll haul in anybody needs haulin'."

"How many need it, Kit?"

"I ain't studied that clear out. If you right about it bein' business, and you may be, nobody needs it." He got up from his chair. "Come on. We'll git to first things first and git you settled in. Then we'll go talk to a couple people and find out if four ears are any better'n two."

FIVE

"You didn't jump up and bust 'im when he was on his way out, did you?" Kit asked Fred as he and I halted in the outer office.

"I by God felt like it," Fred said. "Callin' me a old man. Sonofabitch ain't half the man I am."

"Maybe not a quarter," Kit said.

"Where you off to now?" Fred asked as Kit opened the front door for me.

"Out and around," Kit said. "I'll check in. You keep the radio open."

"Damn thing's always open. Squawk, squawk, and I can't make heads or tails out'n half of the squawks. What you want me to tell 'em when they call in here raisin' hell?"

"Nobody's called in the last hour," Kit said.

"It's a damn plot," Peters said. "They quit when you come in, start in right after you leave."

"Tell 'em what you think they want to hear," Kit said.

"Kit, when you gonna git somebody else in here to answer the phone and do the damn filin' and the rest of the female work and let me git out and git to deputyin' the way I know how to?" Peters asked.

"Right soon now, Fred. Prob'ly 'fore you know it." Kit and I went out into the sun. After a week of cold drizzle in Chicago, the depthless blue sky and the weight of its warmth felt welcome. "Let's take your car," Kit said. We got in. "Old Fred's convinced he is a top-notch detective, and maybe I oughtta let 'im try. Couldn't do no worse'n I been doin'." He directed me south to Catherton's main street and then east on a blacktopped highway, through the fringe of cafés, filling stations and repair shops that ring towns, out to the flat valley floor. Ahead of us a few miles blue-green hills rounded high against the sky, and I knew they fringed Grand Lake. I did as Kit told me several miles later and turned north on a gravel road before we reached the lake, then back east on another, narrower road. We bumped over a six-foot section of two-inch steel pipe laid parallel across the road.

"What's that for—the pipe?" I asked.

"Cattle guard," Kit said. "Space between the pipes, and the cattle can't, or anyway won't, walk across. You Yankees got a lot to learn about decent country."

Trees edged the road thickly as we climbed a long, fast-rising hill, and, when we were over its crest, I saw an A-frame cabin, roofed with heavy-butted shakes, almost hidden by high elms and oaks at its back and its sides. Its back, toward us, blended into the hill's slope, and its sun deck at the front, high on stilts, jutted out toward the lake below us. The road ended in a circle behind the cabin, and I pulled halfway around and stopped the car.

"You home, Jud, if'n it suits you," Kit said. "You like to bring your bag?" I got it from the Corvette while Kit climbed steep steps to the sun deck and unlocked the glass front door. I climbed after him. "Ain't the Pinnacle Club," he said, "but you can prob'ly make do."

I followed him into a paneled room forty feet long and twenty wide. One long wall was centered by a twelve-foot-wide fireplace of rough native stone. Floorboards were wide, pegged and polished oak. A small closed room took up half of the far end of the big room, and, next to it, taking up the other half, was a stainless-steel efficiency kitchen, fronted by a service bar and three plain wooden stools without backs. Two leather-covered easy chairs sagged comfortably behind a heavy oak coffee table in front of the fireplace. A round, scarred wooden poker table with four captain's chairs around it sat toward the front of the room, which was all window and glass door. There were two wide, backless couches along the wall across from the fireplace, covered with red, black, and cream-white Indian blankets. No plastic, chrome or Formica; all wood, stone, leather, steel and heavy cloth; dependable, permanent, comforting substances, a man's house.

"Bath's back there through that door," Kit said. "I turned on the pump and the water heater and stocked up your icebox yestiddy when Jenny cleaned the place up." He wanted me to judge the house and he wanted to judge its effect on me. People who like you and want your approval of something important to them show a certain cautious but eager shyness.

"I ever build a place, it'll be almost exactly like this," I said. "Whose is it, Kit?" I was sure I knew; he had shown his pride in it.

"Mine," he said. "I hoped you'd take to it, even if it ain't fancy and what you used to. Built it about eight years ago, but don't git out here much, not enough; have to stay close to town and trouble. Well, like the Mexicans say, my house is your house." He meant it.

"Thank you, Kit," I said, and I meant that, too.

He helped me put my clothes away in a cedar closet in the corner of the room next to the bath, showed me where things were in the kitchen. "There's beer in the icebox and Jack Daniel's under the bar," he said. "I know you not too strong on moonshine." He said he would show me his fishing dock and his boat later, that I was more than welcome to use them, and he hoped I would if there was time, then gave me the key to the place and we drove back to Catherton.

He didn't talk as we drove, and I knew he was thinking hard on what we had talked about that morning. I wasn't thinking hard, not yet; it was too new to me; there was too much I didn't know, and Kit would tell me what reactions he had to our suppositions when he was ready to tell me. In town, he steered me down one of the streets that stemmed off Main, and we parked in front of a tiny café, got out and went in. An L-shaped counter with nine stools, six in front, three at the end, enclosed a kitchen, and that was all of the café. The place wasn't more than eighteen feet long and ten feet deep. Two men drank coffee at the end of the counter, and Kit nodded to them as he and I sat down at the counter's front. A tall, gaunt, white-haired woman polished the coffee urn across from us. She didn't turn.

"You got people to wait on, old woman," Kit said. "What you got fit to eat?"

"You know, old man," she said, and kept polishing. "Who you got with you?"

"You know that as well as I know you got the same stew you always got on Thursday."

She put down her polishing cloth and turned to us, appraised me openly and carefully. Her eyes flared the same sharp blue as Kit's; she had a wide mouth, tight but quirked with humor, a masculine blade of a nose that

44

would have been too dominant on a face smaller than hers, but one that fit perfectly with her high, wide cheek bones, her strong jaw and her heavy, white eyebrows. She smiled at me, and her face came alive to match her eyes, and I felt suddenly fortunate that I was meeting her. She gave her hand to me, and I took it, warm and tough. "I don't take to last names, Mr. Blade," she said, "so I'll call you Jud. I'm Ma Maxwell, and Kit took a call from you in here the other day. You call me Ma."

"I'll be honored," I said.

"Listen to 'im," she commanded Kit. "Manners might rub off on you."

"I come to eat, old woman, not to listen to you meddle and meander."

The two men down at the end put dimes on the counter and left. She turned with the spare, precise moves of a kitchen expert, took the coins and put them in her apron pocket, picked up the cups and saucers and dropped them in soapy water in a tank behind her, whisked them clean, rinsed them in steaming water in a second tank and stacked them upside down to drain in a wire rack under the counter. She didn't take ten seconds for the whole thing.

"I'll take a Caesar salad, and don't coddle the egg more'n thirty seconds," Kit said. "Go a little heavy on the romaine and a little easy on the iceberg."

"You'll git coddled for more'n thirty seconds," she said. She took two plates and two deep bowls, and, with the same perfect economy of effort, filled them with stew from a huge, heavy iron kettle that sat on the back of the six-burnered stove. "Red top?" she asked.

"Got to git meat in it some way," Kit said.

"What's red top?" I asked.

"Chili on top the stew, Jud," she said. "You better try it that way." She ladled dark red chili over the thickgravied stew and set the plates in front of us, gave us silverware and napkins and a plate of thick-sliced bread. She poured two tall glasses full from a metal pitcher she took from her refrigerator. "Ice-cold buttermilk," she said. "Man like you, Jud, is bound to like ice-cold buttermilk."

"I do," I said. "Thank you."

"Watch 'er, Jud," Kit said. "It is better to mean-mouth 'er. She's actin' too nice for the bossy old woman she is. She'll sneak up on you sudden with a sweet tongue, and first thing you know she'll be bossin' you around the way she tries to boss me but don't. On top of that she knows you ain't married, and there is no tellin' what she has got in her mind about that."

"What you got in your mind today? Any day?" she said.

"Not much. Not enough," Kit said. His words and his thoughts detached him from us; he looked at the exhaust hood across from him, but he didn't see it or anything else.

Ma had gotten busy with a damp cloth, cleaning the counter, and she hadn't seen his mental dismissal of us and his surroundings. "You better git somethin', old man," she said. "People are waitin' for you to make a move of some kind, are sayin' you ought've made one by now."

He heard her and came back; his face tightened and his eyes wintered. He slapped his spoon down. "Damn people and what they say. Damn 'em all," he said explosively. He took a long drink of his buttermilk.

She looked at him quickly and with concern. "Sure, Kit," she said. "I maybe talked out of turn then and I am sorry. I ain't tryin' to push you."

"I didn't mean you," Kit said. "You neither, Jud. You ain't people." He grinned at her and at me, not easily, and she grinned back, then laughed at him. She didn't chuckle; she laughed, loudly and abruptly, the way a man laughs when he slaps down a straight flush against four of a kind.

46

"Got to thinkin' and it strained you and got you on the prod, didn't it, old man?"

"It's your stew, old woman," Kit said. "Would put a goat on the prod."

"Best I've ever eaten," I said, truthfully. Ma smiled at me, the way Kit had smiled when I told him how much I liked his cabin. I had no idea what or how much Kit had told her about me, but she wanted me to like her and to approve of her. She probably had a reason for wanting it, but I felt sure, after knowing her only this long, that it wasn't a selfish reason. I wanted her to like me, too.

"You come in for supper about seven, Jud, alone, and I'll have you a two-pound sirloin, rare, and that salad old sorehead here was talkin' about," Ma said.

"I'll be here."

"There is a lot of talk, Kit, but you know that," she said. "Is there anything new?"

"Only thing is that Jud's here and we been talkin'. I guess now I had better git to doin'."

"Doin' what?"

"Pushin'," he said. "Then pushin' some more, quite a lot more." He had made a decision of some kind, suddenly, probably while he was off in his private distance and depth a minute or two before, and now he felt ready to move on the strength of it. I felt ready to move with him, even if I didn't know the direction; patient waiting, so often effective, didn't seem to apply to this time and these circumstances. "Let's go, Jud. Put it on my tab, Ma." He got through the door and out on the sidewalk before I finished my buttermilk and got off my stool.

"Jud," Ma said to me, "I want somethin' from you. The only way I know is to bust out and ask."

"That's the best way."

"He has told me what you did down here before, what you can do, and he has never had one like this one. He

47

may need a lot of help." She didn't say it dramatically. She had thought this over and had made her own conclusions.

"I'll help if I can," I said.

"He may need somebody to watch out for him."

"I'll try to do that," I said.

"I'll pray for both of you," she said, and I looked at her face and knew that she meant she would get down on her knees. It wasn't a handy phrase; it was her promise.

Kit waited for me in the car. "She tell you to take care of me?" he said.

"Yes."

"You may need to some at that," he said. "Let's us git back to the office; then I will want to go over to the courthouse."

"Bunch of calls, like I told you there'd be," Fred said as we walked through the outer office. "You said tell 'em what they want to hear, so I told two of 'em you was thinkin' of resignin' in the mornin'." He seemed to be back in good humor.

"Fine," Kit said. "I might even do it." From behind his desk, he asked me, "What do you do, Jud, when somebody walks up to you in the street and gives you a flat-handed push in the face?"

"Push back, or get the hell out of the way."

"I am gonna push, and I am not gonna let anybody git outta the way. I will push four, five times if I need to, so this will start a fight, and, when it does, I will know who it is I'm fightin'. That make sense to you?"

I realized what he meant to do.

If Alexander had been killed for business reasons, Kit could force someone to want to kill him for the same reasons. And the someone could be the same someone who killed Alexander. If the killer wasn't the same, he would

48

at least be directed by the same power. It would probably work, and it would also be almost impossible to find a more dangerous way to work.

"Whom do you push, Kit?"

"The people that paid Ben. Who else?"

"How high up does it run?" I asked.

"What do you mean how high?"

"Maybe I mean how low," I said. "Who's running this organization? Is it the people who own the places up at the lake, or is it people out of Kansas City or maybe even Chicago?"

Kit stared hard at me, pushed his chair back and swung his feet to the top of his desk, considered the ceiling. "You talkin' about syndicate," he said. "I hadn't thought about it. I been thinkin' about the boys up there; Jack Simmons heads 'em up, or has been headin' 'em up." He thought awhile longer. "It could be. It could be for damn sure. Slots got to come from somewheres; dice tables come from the same place. It takes connection."

"It could be," I said. "When did the organization start?"

"Like I told you earlier," Kit said, "Ben started takin' a share seven, eight months ago. Must've been about then, a little before. Back a year ago, they was sellin' booze, sure, but they wasn't runnin' anythin' more than a two-bit stud game in a back room. Now it's a lot bigger than that." He shook his head. "In my county." He hated to believe it could be possible. "I am gittin' old."

"It might be local, Kit," I said.

"Might. Might not. Odds are it ain't. Odds are it is syndicate, startin' slow, diggin' in real good, startin' to spread out." He jerked his feet down from the desk, thumped the floor with them. "It don't matter. I made up my mind to push, so I will push."

I do not underestimate the syndicate, which has a great reluctance to kill a lawman, but which has the way and the will to do it if it becomes absolutely necessary. Someone had killed Alexander, and, to me, the killing looked and smelled professional. The syndicate takes as much pride in being professional as the FBI does—and it's hampered a lot less by rules. I wondered if Kit had taken time to think it out to conclusion, if he knew the odds against him if it was syndicate, a small-town sheriff against a shadowy organization so strong, so interwoven internationally that even the FBI didn't know its entire strength and capabilities. I thought, too, of myself. If I committed completely, past the commitment I had already made, there would be two of us against that organization. That shortened the odds mathematically but not realistically, not in any way. Ma would need to pray, hard.

"Where do you push first?" I asked Kit. "Who gets named in the first warrant?"

"You follow me that quick?" he said.

"You realize exactly what you're planning to do?" I asked.

"I got a good idea, Jud. And I will try to do it by myself. I am glad to have you here, but I would a lot rather you stuck to nothin' but the writin' about the end of it—after it's ended."

"If you're bait, Kit, you will need somebody to handle the gaff."

"That ain't your job."

My Maurie once told me that when they made bigger windmills, I would simply get myself a bigger lance. I'm not in Quixote's class as a seeker, but I am out of his class as a doer. Class, presence, pride—call it what you want to—is a quality that each man, if he aspires to it, must try to define for himself to his satisfaction, and there is no satisfaction if he falls short of his definitive self-demand.

"I believe I will make it mine, Kit."

"I got to admit I had counted on it. I told you about the new county attorney?"

"No."

"Commissioners appointed him yestiddy. A boy just started in to practice; nobody else would take it. Name's Billy Joe Briggs. He is scared blue."

"He is probably smart to be scared."

"I talked to 'im 'fore you got here today. I asked 'im if he was gonna take the cash bag when they bring it in the first of the month, and he like to fainted. Said he would run like a jackrabbit in front of a coyote from anybody tried to buy 'im a cuppa coffee."

"Will he give you warrants?"

"I been sheriff here a long time, Jud. He'll give 'em to me or I will tan 'is hide on the third floor of the courthouse, right in front of ever'body, and he knows it. Let's go."

"Maybe I better wait here for you."

"You dealin' yourself in, Jud, I want you to look at the cards right along with me. You got a right."

"It's your town," I said.

We left the building, walked across the street and up the hundred-foot-long walk to the courthouse, rode the painfully slow elevator to the third floor. I remembered our two trips there in June to see Alexander.

"Billy Joe back from lunch, Bessie?" Kit asked. She was the same girl who had been there as Alexander's secretary.

"He's back. Hello, Mr. Blade," she said. "Nice to have you back. Heard you got in this mornin'."

"Thank you," I said.

Kit opened the door to the inner office without knocking, and I followed him in as if I belonged there, too. The man behind the big, glass-topped desk got up quickly and awkwardly from his chair. He looked less like a prosecuting attorney than any I'd ever seen, more like a first-year lawyer jumping to his feet when a Supreme Court justice enters a courtroom. He was tall, an inch or two taller than I, painfully thin. He wore horn-rimmed glasses and had a pleasant, determined face. "Hi, Mr. Marlow," he said.

"Told you to call me Kit, Billy Joe. This here is Jud Blade, a good friend of mine."

"Bessie told me. How do you do, Mr. Blade."

"Fine, thank you, Mr. Briggs." We shook hands. He had a surprisingly strong grip.

"Billy Joe, you fix me up a warrant to raid Annie's tonight. No, make that tomorrow mornin'. Doesn't git goin' good out there till maybe one or two o'clock," Kit said.

The boy's eyes widened a little and he swallowed hard, twice. "How come, Mr. Marlow?"

"She is operatin' a disorderly house. She is sellin' booze. They is gamblin'. She is a disgrace to the community and I aim to close 'er up."

"She's been doin' it for two, three years," Briggs said.

"She has got one girl out there now ain't more'n sixteen," Kit said. "I won't have that kind of thing in this county. Fix me up the warrant."

"You know what you're doin'?"

"I know," Kit said.

"She'll be out on bail before you get her locked up good," Briggs said.

"I know that, too. She is, and I'll raid 'er agin tomorrow night. I will also be wantin' some other warrants for some other places."

"Which other places?" Briggs sat down and tried to bring this into focus.

"I ain't absolutely sure," Kit said. "That dance hall boat up on the lake, the Paradise Club, Blaine's, the Indian Inn, maybe a couple others."

"Holy Jesus," Briggs said.

"I'll let it get out good, Billy Joe, that this is my doin', not yours," Kit said.

"You don't do that, I'll have to," Briggs said. "You are stompin' on some mighty big toes."

"I aim to," Kit said.

"Just the one for Annie's today?"

"That's all. We'll start fairly small."

"I'll send it over to you in an hour or so," Briggs said.

"I'll expect it," Kit said. He started out, and I nodded to Briggs and said I had been pleased to meet him.

"Mr. Marlow, you sure?" Briggs said when Kit was at the door.

"I'm sure, Billy Joe. And thank you."

"I guess you're welcome."

When we were back out on the sidewalk I asked Kit about Annie's.

"Late-hours place, a private club," he said. "Annie is rough, rough as they come, but up until three, four months ago, she run a fair place. A man could git a drink, dance a time or two, maybe find a fairly friendly game. Now she has got three girls out there used to be amateurs and have turned professional. One of 'em ain't over sixteen. And I hear the game has got big and unfriendly. Somebody has organized old Annie, and I aim to flush out who."

"This is the hard way," I said.

"It's the fastest and the surest, maybe the onliest."

"That it is."

"Jud, I got to go talk to some people. I am still not th'owin' away the idea that whoever killed Ben and Beth done it for revenge on Ben."

"It could be, Kit."

"These people don't cotton none to strangers, so I won't ask you along."

"Can I go along tonight?" I asked.

53

"You want to?"

"Sure. You said I could see the cards when they're dealt."

"All right," Kit said. "Be at the office around midnight."

"I'll be there."

I drove back to the cabin, wondering all the way if this trip—trip twenty-one—would be the last I'd take.

SIX

The quiet at the cabin that afternoon should have been soporific, but it had the opposite effect; my senses strained and sharpened. I'm not used to natural sounds; light wind in thick-leaved trees, slight rustle back in dense brush that, relatively, is as sudden as the backfire of a truck engine in a city, faint dog bark somewhere far over the hill. A small-screen television set sat at the end of the service bar, next to the telephone, but I didn't turn it on. Every man has some Thoreau in him; maybe mine would have its first chance to emerge.

I sat in one of the big easy chairs, shoes off and feet up on the coffee table, which, judging by its scars, had accepted feet often, and wondered about this trip: the day, Ma Maxwell, Kit's sudden decision that I was right about the cause of the killings and that he had to precipitate revelatory action; about Pat and the relationship she and I have and where that will end; about Maurie and me and

55

the almost two years of joy and sweetness she and I had together, that I'll never have again; about myself.

I'm well acquainted with the fascination of introspection, but I try usually not to indulge it, so I forced my mind back to the reason I had come here, a rape and two murders, to what I had found and learned. Some. Not enough to select a course for myself.

Either someone local, for private reasons, had killed Alexander and raped and killed his girl, or someone had killed him for business reasons, raped and killed her because she happened to be there. If it were the former, I would have to rely on Kit, and Kit had decided it wasn't. If it were the latter, and if Kit pushed hard enough, I'd find out more the fast, hard way, when Kit got his return push. Would I be able to counter, to do anything? Would there be help from Mercer and James? They seemed to be traveling their own paths, apart from Kit. Did they sense syndicate? Did it make sense for me to feel it? We'd start to find out tonight. My thoughts circled, ran back into themselves.

I awoke. Could it be six-thirty? My watch said so. I got up and walked to the sun deck. The wind had quieted, and the lake lay stilled, its blue darkening in anticipation of evening. I walked down the graveled path to Kit's corrugated-tin boat house. He had a fourteen-foot fishing boat, contoured swivel chairs mounted fore and aft, fitted with a twenty-five horse engine. Everyone says motor, but it's an engine; I learned that in the Air Corps. Rods and reels, six of them of different styles and sizes, were racked neatly in brackets along one wall of the boathouse. Kit apparently took fishing seriously. I don't know much about it, but I hoped he and I would get a chance to try. This kind of living appealed to me and I'd never had a chance to sample it seriously. Maybe when this trip ended. I felt the promise of autumn, went back up to the cabin, put on a sports coat, climbed into the Corvette, and drove to Catherton, not hurrying. The afternoon had taken the hurry out of me.

"I was beginning to think you didn't want the steak," Ma said when I took a stool at the end of the cramped room. Three men at the other end were finishing coffee after their dinners.

"You said two pounds, rare," I said.

"Well, a pound and a half, anyway." She began to heat a heavy iron skillet. "Fresh out of charcoal," she said.

The three men shoved back their cups and stood. Ma took money from one of them and gave him change, lifted the hinged section of the counter and came through. She locked the door behind them and pulled shades at it and at the window.

"You close early," I said.

"Best chance I've had in three years and seven months to be alone with a young buck like you," she said. She went back behind the counter, dipped a finger in a glass and shook a drop of water onto the skillet. It sizzled. "Not hot enough; got to bounce," she said. She took a salad from her refrigerator, peppered it, blended oil and wine vinegar from separate cruets on it, and put it in front of me. "Ain't a Caesar, since I don't know exactly how to make one, but it'll have to do."

The lettuce was all crisp green, no white, and the tomatoes were firm and meaty, the slices of radish white and hard. "It'll do," I said. She gave me silverware, tested the skillet again. The drop bounced and became steam. She took the steak, an inch and a half thick, seven or eight inches in diameter, from the back of her cutting board where she had been warming it and slapped it into the skillet. "That all for me?"

"You a growed-up man," she said. "Need a growed-up meal. Can't stand a finicky eater. Don't trust one."

"You'll trust me then," I said.

"Already do."

"Thank you, Ma." The salad tasted as good as it looked. I ate about half of it before she turned the steak. "Has Kit been in for dinner?"

"Won't be in," she said. "He's nosin' around in the hills up north, stirrin' up God knows how many hornets' nests."

"You keep pretty good track of him."

"Somebody needs to." She took a huge baked potato out of her oven, put it on a separate plate and peeled back its foil, sliced it up the middle, pushed both ends with her big, competent red hands, crumpled it perfectly. She put it in front of me, along with a plate of sliced butter, then lifted the steak to a platter and served that. "You eat now. We'll talk later."

I ate and hadn't realized I was so hungry. She cleaned her kitchen and we finished at about the same time. She poured coffee for both of us.

"Best I've had since noon," I said.

"You prob'ly used to better."

"There isn't any better."

"Me and my kitchen staff thank you. I come on kind of sudden with you at noon, Jud, tellin' you Kit needs help and askin' you to give it."

"Not too sudden."

"I ain't sure Kit knows how deep the water is likely to git."

"Do you know, Ma?"

"No. I hear a lot in here, more'n you'd ever think. I know who is moonshinin' and who is buyin' sugar and gittin' ready to, who's fixin' to bust whose head, who's sleepin' with who, but this time—this thing about Ben and Beth—I ain't heard anything but a lot of loose and nervous talk about nearly nothin'. I know this, though:

58

Kit decided today, while you and him was in here, that he's gonna do somethin', and when Kit decides that, somethin' gits done, one way or another."

"You know him pretty well," I said.

"I'm his friend," she said. "If I was ten years younger, I'd be his wife. Make it five." She looked at me directly and said it proudly, then grinned at her seriousness. "I was twenty years younger, I'd aim after you."

"I'd be proud," I said.

"You and him got somethin' on for tonight?"

"Yes, we have."

"It figgers. I don't aim to pry. May want to but I won't."

I trusted this woman completely, the same way I had trusted Kit a half hour after I had met him, but I had no reason to tell her Kit's plans and I have a rule: have a reason. "I'll get out and let you close clear up, Ma."

She laughed, abruptly, as she had at lunch. "You go on," she said. "You just told yourself old Ma is like all wimmen, sayin' she won't, which means she will if you don't get away from 'er." She again came through the counter, unlocked the door.

"How much do I owe you?" I asked.

"Told you to go on," she said. "First steak is on the house."

"I wouldn't feel . . ."

"You argue with me, I'll quit cookin' for you. I'll see you tomorrow. Be careful."

"Thanks."

"You welcome, Jud." She pulled the café door to behind me.

Kit had said midnight, and my watch said a little after eight. I could have stayed and talked with Ma, but it is never wise to hurry a friendship; one must grow of itself, and both persons need to recognize and accept that if the growth is to be successful. I left the Corvette at the curb and walked toward Main Street. Have you ever walked at night in a small town? The sidewalks stretch wide and clean but cracked and weary. Shop windows glow dimly; they don't glitter, and their displays are crowded staticly, as though their arrangers, not confident of quality or aware of the lack of it, use quantity as a compromise. I met only one man, and he looked at me with open curiosity and said, "Hi, fine evening," and I agreed it was. With all the quiet I didn't feel lonely, but then I've been a loner all of my life except for the time with Maurie and the interrupted times with Pat, and loners either don't get lonely or accept being so as a natural, usually even agreeable, way of life. Fluorescent lights outlined a movie; I hadn't seen one in eight or nine years, so I gave a dollar to the cashier, a middle-aged woman who didn't look up from her magazine while she tore off a ticket from a roll and then tore it in two and gave me half; no usher. Probably two dozen people shared the theater with me. For more than two hours I watched John Wayne, who hit people in the head with his rifle barrel, a big improvement in reality; movie stars used to hit people in the head with their hands, and there's no better way to break hands and lose a fight. The throat or the belly if you have to use your fists. Wayne won; the lights went up; Catherton's night life, the surface portion of it, ended. I went back to my Corvette and drove to the City-County building. Fred sat at his desk in the outer office, his elbow propped on the desk top, his head propped on his hand. He jerked upright when I closed the door behind me. "I wake you up, Fred?"

"I was thinkin'," he said.

"You work all the time?" I asked.

"Might' near. Chief, the other jailer, got sick and went home. You been out livin' it up?"

"Been deputyin' for John Wayne," I said.

"I seen it. He busts them heads, don't he? Maybe we oughtta bust a few around here, find out a few things the easy way. You found out anything, Blade?"

"About what?"

"Well, hell, now. You like Kit; think I'm good for nothin' but answerin' the damn phone and fillin' out forms. You know about what." He snorted at me disgustedly.

"I haven't found out anything, Fred."

"You writers supposed to be smarter'n us hick laws. Ever' story I ever read you was."

"That's because writers write the stories."

"Figgered that," he said.

"You found out anything?" I asked.

"I am workin' on it. Lot of things don't match up the way they oughtta. You didn't know Ben too well, did you?"

"No."

"I knowed 'im since he was borned. Ben was careful and he was smart. Kept records on ever damn thing, always writin' notes to hisself, always dictatin', but when that state boy opened the vault over there, he didn't find much of nothin'. Somewheres Ben left a bunch of facts. I will bet a forty-dollar hat against a dime cigar that somewheres in them facts is a clue." His old hawk's face showed the intensity of his conviction.

"Did Kit search his house?"

"Kit went over it good. The state boys've been over it until they know ever' cockroach by its first name."

"Then there must be nothing."

"Goddlemighty, Blade, just because nobody's found nothin' don't prove they ain't somethin'. I aim to have me a try."

"How, Fred?"

"I got tomorry off. I will . . . never you mind. I'll do 'er myself." He got up from his chair and walked to the counter, poured himself a mug of coffee that was so black it looked viscous. "And when I do 'er, I'll git out from behind this damn desk."

Car lights pulled up to the curb outside and then went out. Kit came up the walk and into the room. "Shooo," he said. "Long day. How come you're here, Fred? Where's Chief?"

"Got sick. Went home."

"Bad sick?"

"Nah. He et too much."

"When you gonna sleep?"

"Frank'll be in at six and I'm off tomorry."

"I appreciate it." He poured a cup of coffee. "You can go back in one of the cell beds after Jud and me are gone."

"Where you goin'?" Peters asked.

"Billy Joe send somethin' over for me?"

"Yeah. In a envelope. It's on your desk. I couldn't see through to find out what it was."

"I bet you tried," Kit said.

"Damn right. A undersheriff has got to be informed. What is it?"

"You sleep all afternoon, Jud?" Kit asked.

"It's quiet out there," I said.

"Quiet here, too. Let's git off our butts and stir it up some."

"How?" Peters asked. "Where you goin', Kit?"

"Callin' on a girl friend of yours. Old Annie." He put down the coffee cup and went to his office, came back tearing open an envelope. "Got me a warrant here."

"You gonna raid old Annie?"

"It ain't a social call," Kit said.

"How come, Kit?"

"Figger it's past time."

Peters jutted his head out on his long, corded neck, stared at Kit. "You put enough pressure on a old boiler and she'll blow out at 'er thinnest spot, won't she?" I could almost watch the connections make themselves in his brain. "Yessir, she sure as hell will."

"Sure as hell," Kit said. "Come on, Jud."

"She hides the booze in her kitchen, in the oven," Peters said.

"I know that," Kit said.

"You gonna bring her in?"

"Sure."

"I'll fix a bed in the padded cell. Mad as Annie'll git, she'll be better off in there."

"You do that, Fred," Kit said. He and I left.

"We'll take my car," he told me, "because we will need a back seat comin' back, but when we park out there, I'll scrooch down so nobody sees me if they look out. You go to the door; they keep it locked. Tell 'em you on your way to Tulsa from the lake and have heard you could git a drink there—No. Say you've got one there before. Otis will be too dumb to think who you might be. I'll give you five minutes or so and then bang on the door. Save that drink; they ain't supposed to serve no one except out of his own bottle. If I ask you if they sold it to you, you tell me they did. All right?"

"Fine, Kit."

He drove west to the highway, then south past Catherton's limit sign. Annie's was a low, long ranch house set back forty or fifty feet from the highway. A small blue neon sign over the front door said PRIVATE CLUB. Six or seven cars were parked in the gravel lot in front of the house and Kit pulled close in behind one. I got out of the car, walked to the front door and tried the knob; it was locked, so I knocked. The door opened the length of a lock chain, and a tired man's face above heavy shoulders asked me if I was a member.

"No," I said, "but I've been here before, two, three times. I'm driving back from the lake to Tulsa, and it's too late to get a bottle."

He didn't even look carefully at me. He took the chain loose and let me in, led the way to the bar. "What'll you have?"

"Bourbon and water."

"Good. We just run outta scotch." He mixed a thin drink and put it in front of me. "Dollar," he said. I paid him and tasted the drink. Fair floor varnish. The bar ran down one long side of the rectangular room. Booths were built into the opposite wall and one end wall. Annie believed in darkness for decoration. I could see shadows of people in two of the booths across from me, a lighted cigarette tip in one of the booths at the end of the room. A jukebox near the door I had entered provided most of the light, that and a shaded lamp on the back bar. There was a small dance floor. The one big room didn't take up more than a fourth of the house. I wondered what the rest of it held.

Kit's knock was peremptory. The bartender–receptionist didn't hurry to the door, but, after he had opened it, he hurried to slam it. "Marlow," he yelled. He ran back to the bar, scooped up three or four bottles and carried them through a door at the back end of the bar. The lighted cigarette in the far booth hurried to a door at the end of the room, disappeared briefly, returned and came toward and then past me. I saw that it was in the mouth of a short, wide woman; she rolled when she walked. Kit banged harder on the door. She turned the knob and opened it, kept the chain on. "What the hell you want?" she said

"In," Kit said.

"You ain't a member. This here is a private club."

"And this here is a warrant to raid this here private club," Kit said. "Open 'er up, Annie."

"You bastard," she said. "I ain't supposed to git raided."

"Nobody told me. Open up."

Four men came out of the door Annie had come through a minute before, sat in two of the booths. A small woman followed seconds later, joined two of them. Annie fumbled at the chain. "Stuck," she said.

"Unstick it in a hurry," Kit said. She looked around the room, then opened the door. Kit came in. "Lights, Annie."

She reached along the wall and flipped a switch. I blinked in the sudden light from overhead bulbs. The shabbiness of the room jumped out at me. Bilious green plastic, scarred and patched, covered the booths. The walls were scabrous plasterboard. The hardwood floorboards of the dance floor hadn't been waxed since God knew when; they looked like duckboards in a shower room. The people in the booths, twelve in all, stared fixedly at each other and at tabletops. They didn't turn their heads toward Kit. The woman who had come into the room from the end door wasn't a woman; she was a girl: black hair, shadowed eyes, heavily made up, lipstick a scarlet slash across her thin face.

"Where'd Otis go, Annie?" Kit asked.

"Back to the john," she said. She wore a shapeless print housedress and flat bedroom slippers. She wasn't more than five feet two inches tall, but she must have weighed a hundred and sixty or seventy. Whatever she had been and had known hadn't ravaged her face; it had destroyed it. "What the hell is this, Marlow? I got a license."

"Only for some things, Annie," Kit said. "You can yell

in to Otis and tell 'im not to bother puttin' your booze in the oven. I ain't after that."

"That's private stock back there," she said. "I got a right to private stock, same as any citizen."

"Sure you do," Kit said. He walked up to me. "You buy that drink here or did you bring your own bottle?"

"I bought it here," I said.

"You fink sonofabitch," Annie screamed at me.

"He's a friend of mine," Kit told her. He took a small plastic bag and rubber bands from his pocket, put the bag over the top of my glass and secured it with the bands. "I need 'im to, he'll testify." He walked to the booth that held the girl. "You Dorothy Sullens, ain't you?"

She glared up at him, didn't answer or nod. The man sitting next to her said, " She just came up here and sat down with us when you came to the door. We don't know her." He had panic in his voice.

"Come on, Dorothy," Kit said. "You and Annie and me goin' into town."

"Goddamn you, Marlow, she lives here," Annie said. "She didn't have no home and I took 'er in."

Kit ignored her. "Rest of you can go on home," he told the people in the booths. "This place is closed."

Seven men and two women probably broke some sort of record for leaving a room. Two women, both young, stayed, their tired, defeated faces emotionless. Annie waved her hand at them. "They waitresses," she said. "Live in the back."

"You got you quite a household, Annie," Kit said. "Well, they look old enough. They can stay here and keep Otis company, seein' as how he is gonna git lonesome without no customers. From now on, no customers."

"You sonofabitch, I'll be back open tomorrow night," she said.

"Jail's open now," Kit said. "You and Dorothy come on along."

SEVEN
☩☩☩☩☩☩☩☩☩☩☩☩☩

I came awake quickly and completely Friday morning, and it seemed strange and pleasant to hear no city sounds, no movement outside; I doubted that anyone lived within a mile or two of the cabin. I showered and shaved in the bathroom that Kit had made as modern as Hilton's newest and best, perked coffee in the shining, compact kitchen, and drank it while I sat in my shorts in a canvas chair on the sun deck.

Kit and Fred had put Annie and the Sullens girl in a single cell that made up the women's side of the Catherton jail. Annie's profanity by the time the cell door closed behind her would have made a hard-core pornographer wince. What was it Peters had cackled? "She sounds meaner'n nine miles of muddy road." The Sullens girl had never said a word, even when Kit questioned her, politely and gently, but she hadn't seemed frightened or apprehensive, only defiant. I looked at my watch: ten-thirty. It had been almost five when I got to bed, but five or six hours sleep is all I need. I had another cup of coffee, dressed, and drove to Catherton and to the City–County building. Kit and another man I recognized but whose name I couldn't remember were in the outer office.

"Mornin'," I said. It's the standard greeting in Oklahoma.

"Mornin'," Kit said. "Jud, you remember Frank Butler, my deputy."

"Sure," I said. "Hi, Frank." We shook hands. He was about twenty-five, hard and stocky, dressed like Kit in faded khakis, but he wore a black, glossy-shined gunbelt that held gleaming cartridges and what looked like the big magnum. I had met him briefly in June.

"Hello, Mr. Blade," he said.

"Thought you was gonna sleep all day," Kit said. "Ma wondered how come you didn't make it in for breakfast. She's worried you ain't eatin' right."

"Managed to sleep most of it. Don't eat breakfast," I said. "How's Annie this morning?"

"Freer'n a bird," he said. "Took 'er over to arraignment 'bout a hour ago. Charged 'er with contributin' to delinquency and with sellin' liquor. She said she wasn't guilty, and Judge Johnson set 'er bail at a thousand five hunderd on each charge. Sam Ballard put up bail, and she left the same way she come in—cussin' me."

"What about the girl?"

"Ward of the court. She is over to the doctor's now, and then one of them wimmen at the Welfare Department will take 'er down to the State Home at Carroll City. Damn shame. Folks're dead and she'd been livin' with a no-good aunt until she went out to Annie's. There is no tellin' what the doctor'll find. I should'a gone out there quicker. Should'a done quite a damn few things quicker, Jud." He looked away at the wall and shook his head.

"A man does what he can, Mr. Marlow," Frank said.

"A man does what needs doin'," Kit said. "What the hell is this?"

Haley Mercer and Don James half carried, half dragged a man through the door and past the counter. They sat him down roughly in the folding metal chair across the desk from Frank. His hands were cuffed behind him, but he tried to kick at Mercer when he had his balance on the chair. Mercer stepped back easily, then quite calmly and precisely kicked back. His shoe point popped the man's shin. The man grunted and glared out of one good eye. He said, "I aim to kill you sonsabitches. You better go ahead and kill me now while you got the chance, because I will kill both of you when I git mine." His other eyed had puffed shut, the skin shiny and purpling above a misshapen cheek. His broken lower lip protruded and warped his mouth into a clumsy snarl. Blood had dried down one side of his jaw where it had run from the top of his ear, which had been torn a quarter of an inch away from his head. Mucus and blood had dried on his upper lip. What was left of his face looked Indian, and his long, wild hair, matted above the torn ear, was as blue-black as crow feathers, but the open eye flared blue hate, and Indians do not have blue eyes. He was probably in his mid-forties, not tall but very wide, almost no neck, sloped, muscle-bunched shoulders. He wore a faded blue work shirt, ripped at one shoulder, old blue jeans and scuffed work shoes. He tried to wipe his upper lip with his shoulder, but the cuffs wouldn't allow him enough movement.

"That's what you told Alexander," Mercer said, "but you have done your killin'. You are through." He had a vivid welt across his left cheekbone and he cradled a swelling right hand to his stomach. James showed no marks.

"All right, Mercer," Kit said. "How come?"

"You, too, Marlow, goddamn you," the man said. "You knowed where I was, and I told you yestiddy I'd stay there. You, too."

"Shut up, Tug," Kit said. "How come, Mercer?"

"How come?" Mercer said. "How come you hadn't told us about him and Alexander? How come you hadn't already brought him in? How come we had to find out for ourselves he tried two months ago to kill Alexander and swore he would kill him next time he got a chance, same as he just now swore he'd kill me? He's guilty as hell; that's how come." He turned to Frank. "Here's the key to the cuffs. Put him in a cell by himself." Frank looked at Kit for authority.

"Go ahead, Frank," Kit said. "Then call Doc Shute. Nose is broke, and he'll need a coupla stitches in that ear."

The man got up unsteadily from his chair. He braced himself and turned his back to Frank. "Take 'em off in here," he said. "Give me one more chance at the sonsabitches."

Mercer reached his left hand to his back pocket and brought out a flat leather sap, stained with blackened blood. "You'll git carried back, you half-breed bastard," he said.

Kit moved easily, quickly, and caught Mercer's arm. "Been enough of that already," he said. "You go with Frank, Tug."

The man hunched his shoulders forward, stared at Kit, and grunted out something in a guttural, sliding language. I knew enough from my June trip to know he spoke Cherokee. Kit answered him in Cherokee. He turned and walked slowly through the door and into the hall that led to the jail section of the building. Frank followed him. Mercer put the sap back in his pocket and slumped down on one corner of the desk, still babying his right hand.

70

"You bust it, Haley?" James asked.

"Don't know." He tested the knuckles with his left thumb. "Prob'ly just jammed."

"Tug's got a right hard head," Kit said. "You boys been busy this mornin'." His voice was even and pleasant; his eyes weren't.

"We got started early," Mercer said. "Why didn't you tell us about him, Marlow?" He was making his effort to be pleasant, too. He looked satisfied in spite of his injured hand.

"Got the list you asked for in there on my desk," Kit said. "His name's on the top of it. I talked to 'im yestiddy afternoon, but I didn't believe I had enough to bring 'im in. You must've thought different."

"We talked to Alexander's secretary—Briggs's now— first thing when we got here this mornin'. She told us about Wilson and his trouble with Alexander, about how Wilson swore he'd kill him, so we drove out there to talk. We're lucky we got back with him. Should've shot him," Mercer said.

"We told him we were going to bring him in, and he tried to get in the house to get his gun," James said. "Haley had to bust him."

"Finally had to use my sap on him," Mercer said. "Get the stuff out of the car, Don."

James went out, came back in a minute with a pump shotgun, a box of shells, a pair of hunting boots. He put them on the desk in front of Kit.

"Twelve gauge," Mercer said. "And the shells, same brand and same color, are number fours, same shot we got out of the bodies, and there are three gone out of the box, exactly three. We checked the boot soles against the plaster cast we took out at Alexander's. Perfect match. And a man don't fight arrest like that unless he's guilty. I figure that gives us enough." He started to get a cigarette

71

from his shirt pocket with his bad hand, winced, reached with his left hand. James lighted it for him. "We'll find out where he was Sunday, and I'll bet he's got no alibi. Whatever more we need, we'll get it. We've got your killer for you, Marlow."

"I ain't sure it's enough," Kit said. "We'll have to go see Billy Joe."

"We got resisting arrest until we get enough for murder one, if we need any more, which I don't figure we do," James said.

A tall, thin man, carrying a doctor's bag, came through the door. "Where is he, Kit?" he said. "I'm busy as hell, but Frank said he's half dead. Who is it?"

"Tug Wilson. You know 'im."

"Couldn't kill Tug with an ax," the doctor said.

"Look at this man's hand first, Doc," Kit said.

Mercer held out his hand, half again as thick through the knuckles as it should have been. The doctor took it, tested the puffiness with his thumb. "You must've hit Tug in the head," he said.

"Did," Mercer said.

"Prob'ly broken then. I'll have to have a picture. Know where the hospital is?"

"We'll find it," James said.

"Get over there and get ice on it before it gets as big as a basketball," the doctor said. "Tug in the back, Kit?"

"Frank's back there with 'im," Kit said. "You know the way." The doctor went down the hall.

"I guess we better get over there," Mercer said.

"Straight out east on Main Street," Kit said.

"Back as soon as we can," James said.

"Sure," Kit said. They left. Kit went to the counter and poured coffee for both of us, handed me one mug, and led the way to his office. "They worked 'im over pretty fair, didn't they? I don't hold with that."

"Sometimes it has to be done," I said.

"One lick with that sap would have been enough. Looks to me they kept on takin' licks."

"A man can get pretty mad," I said. I remembered a time or two when I had. I'm not proud of it, but it happens to every man who enforces the law. The thing is never to let it become a method or a habit.

"Sure," he said.

"I feel damned unnecessary around here now," I said.

"I don't think Tug done it," Kit said.

"That doesn't sound like a sheriff."

"Can't help how it sounds."

"What was Mercer talking about, Kit, when he said this Wilson threatened to kill Alexander?"

"I should've told you yestiddy. 'Bout two months ago I arrested Tug's son, boy named Caleb, on assault and battery. Tug held the boy had been in a fair fight, but Ben had a signed complaint, so he filed on the boy after I brought 'im in. Tug went up to talk to Ben about it, lost 'is head, and wound up hittin' Ben in the eye, threatenin' to kill 'im. Spent the night in jail here, and next day he and Ben shook hands, and that was all there was to it."

"He hit the county attorney?"

"Tug's got a hot head."

"And Ben didn't prosecute him?"

"No. Ben said he'd egged Tug on, not meanin' to," Kit said.

"I'll be damned. I am never going to understand you people."

"Told you you got to grow up here."

"But Wilson did threaten to kill Ben?" I asked.

"While he was fightin' mad," Kit said. "He apologized for it. Even said Ben had done what he had to do and he would vote for 'im next election."

"Why don't you think he did it?" I asked. "When you and I first talked about this, you believed someone from around here killed Ben for a reason like the one Wilson has."

"I decided different. You decided me. You want a drink of this here backwoods sippin' whiskey?" He reached down and got his bottle.

"No thanks, Kit."

"Believe I'll have a small one." He did. "Tug might kill somebody while he was mad. He wouldn't plan a killin' and wait behind a tree to do it. And he ain't a rapist. He just ain't that kind. I've knowed 'im for twenty years."

"Mercer said the shells matched. The shot size matched. The boots matched."

"I ain't a lawyer, but you know that is circumstantial," Kit said. He put the bottle back in its drawer. "Ever'body hunts ducks has got number four shells, and half the shells sold around here are that brand. Three of 'em ain't no magic number. Tug's boots is normal size, and they is a lot of normal-sized men."

The doctor opened the door and stuck his head in. "Fixed him up, Kit," he said. "I'll send the county the bill."

"You do that, Doc. He hurt much?"

"Nose is broken. Been broken three, four times before, so I couldn't do anything about it. Stitched his ear and his head. Good as new in a few days." He closed the door and left.

"Be a lot easier for you if Wilson is the one who did it," I told Kit.

"It bein' easy don't make it right," Kit said. "I don't think he done it."

"What did he tell you in Cherokee?"

"He didn't ask me what we are havin' for lunch."

74

"How much Indian is he?" I asked.

"More'n half, and the rest is Irish; that mix makes 'im hotter'n a two-dollar pistol shootin' downhill on the Fourth of July. He lives over north and east and don't hardly ever come outta the hills. I said I saw 'im yestiddy, and, when I did, he told me he didn't know nothin' about Ben's gittin' shot, that him and Ben was good friends."

"After he busted Ben?"

"Some of the best friends I know got that way after they had pounded on each other and then shook hands."

"Where do we go from here, Kit?"

Butler put his head in the door and said, "Guess who you got for a visitor?"

"The counselor? Already?"

"Already."

Kit turned to me. "Old beer joint buddy of yours. Tug is one of his clients. Send 'im on in, Frank."

Swimmer Early, all six feet eight and three hundred pounds of him—and those estimates are as conservative as a Boston-born John Bircher—made it through the door, barely. His size and his appearance shrank doors, rooms, and other people. Swimmer is a full-blooded Cherokee and a highly capable lawyer. He and I had gotten to know each other in June. I had seen him in action stopping a beer joint knife fight; he ended up with both knives, which he broke in his hands the way I would break a pencil. I had been able to do him a favor by throwing my knife at the right time at one of the belligerents who planned to use his blade on Swimmer's back. I respected him, his tremendous strength and the gentleness with which he used it unless he needed to unleash it. I liked his sense of humor, his pragmatic philosophies, and his aims, which were to better the lives and lots of the Cherokees, and I liked him, as well as, maybe better than I have ever liked anyone. He needed only two steps to put his bulk up against the front of Kit's desk. "This county has finally gone clear to hell," he bellowed, "and I have come to wreck and destroy this sorry, stinkin' den of perdition." He raised a fist that looked like a knotty basketball and slammed it down on the desk top, which I expected to fold and collapse. "Citizens are gittin' beat on. Come out from under that desk and be the first to pay for your terrible sins."

Kit stood up and shoved back his chair, leaned forward and yelled back. "I will put you so far back in jail beans will have to be shot to you with a cannon. I smell vile moonshine on your heathen Indian breath."

"Come out from there so I can pull a arm off at a time," Swimmer boomed. He reached across the desk, grabbed one of Kit's shoulders in each hand and lifted him a foot off the floor.

"A hunderd and forty years for assault with intent to kill a white man while filthy drunk on illegal moonshine booze," Kit yelled. "Maybe two hunderd and forty. Shoot 'im in both legs, Blade. I want 'im left alive to suffer."

Swimmer put him down gently, turned to face me. "White-eyes with forked pen," he said. "I will kill the high sheriff after I have settled scores with you." He started for me.

I jumped up from my chair and pushed up to him. When you're as big as I am, it is ridiculous to feel physically inadequate. Swimmer stuck his huge belly out and bumped me about a foot. I set my left foot out and slammed a hook into his belly. I pulled it, but not too much. I've knocked men down with a punch that good. I rejoiced immediately over the fact that I hadn't hit him harder; I would probably have broken a hand. I jumped back and raised my hands, palms out.

"You got that sword hiked up on the back of your neck?" he asked

76

"And a forty-five in each side pocket, plus hand grenades on each hip," I said. That's the kind of armament you'd need to go up against Swimmer.

"Then I am goin' off the warpath. I am glad to see you, Jud." He put out his hand, and I shook it. "Heard you come back. The thing about Beth and Ben was terrible." He turned to Kit, the horseplay over, his broad, flat face impassive. "This thing about Tug is bad, too. He hurt much?"

"Tug's all right, Swimmer," Kit said. He sat back down. I took a chair and Swimmer did, too. It disappeared when he sat on it. "Doc Shute took care of 'im." He rubbed one of his shoulders. "Be a little damn careful next time. You like to crippled me."

"You told Tug yesterday you didn't need him in here, and he told you he'd stay where he was in case you wanted him," Swimmer said. He didn't make an accusation; it sounded like a question.

"I told 'im that," Kit said. "I don't hold none with what happened this mornin', but them state boys didn't bother to ask me." He didn't excuse himself; he made a flat, truthful statement.

"I know you better'n to think it was your doin'," Swimmer said.

"You'd better bet your aborigine ass you do," Kit said.

"I misdoubt you know what the word means," Swimmer said.

"A ass is what lawyers generally make out of themselves."

"Second only to sheriffs," Swimmer said. "And sheriffs is second only to writers."

"Where does an oversized blanket-ass rank?" I asked.

"I told you I am scared of you," Swimmer said.

"You want to see Tug, Swimmer?" Kit asked.

"No need right now, long as you say he's all right. You think Tug did it, Kit?"

"No."

"How come the state boys do?"

Kit told him about the shells, the boot prints and the gun. "And they heard about the fuss Tug had with Ben up in the courthouse," he said.

"That isn't enough," Swimmer said.

"They think it is."

"Will Billy Joe file on him?"

"Good chance he will," Kit said. "Billy Joe is bound to be pretty impressed by the state boys."

"I better start doin' my homework," Swimmer said. "I will admit to you I don't know where Tug was Sunday evenin'. I don't know what we got for an alibi, but if they file, I know we will beat it." He got up from the chair. "Jud, you want to go drink a beer or three tonight?"

"What do you have on?" I asked Kit.

"Same thing as last night," he said.

"Annie's?" Swimmer asked. "You know what you're doin', Kit?"

"I know."

"Need any help?"

"Might at that. I do, I'll ask."

"I believe I will go along with Kit tonight," I told Swimmer. Kit had taken a snapping turtle's hold on the idea that he could and would force someone's hand, and I had begun it for him. I had also told Ma that I would be around to watch him and take care of him. It felt like a strange role for me. I work better when I watch enemies and potential enemies, take care of myself and spend no time worrying about taking care of anyone else, but I had accepted the role. I would play it.

"Somebody had better," Swimmer said. "I am glad it's you." He shook hands with me again preparatory to leaving. My hand is big; it disappeared inside his. "I'll check with you on Tug late this afternoon or first thing in the mornin'," he told Kit. He left. I've never seen a grizzly bear charge, but the thought came to me that Swimmer must move like one, powerfully, imperviously, but somehow daintily. Very good heavyweights and the best running backs move that way.

"Then we're going back to Annie's," I said.

"Figger we might as well," Kit said.

"I'll never get in or get a drink tonight."

"We'll go in different. Sudden," Kit said. "Now I don't wanta run you off, Jud, but I got me some things to do. I got to talk to Tug; he'll be cooled off enough now, but he won't say a damn word with you around. Then I got to go see Billy Joe about Tug and about gittin' another warrant for tonight, although I don't really give a damn if'n I have one. You show up about the same time as last night."

"I'm getting too much rest," I said.

"They ain't any such thing as too much rest. I aim to git me some before we start out tonight."

I ate lunch at Ma's, but I got in during the noon rush hour, when there were people waiting behind each stool, and she and I had no time to ourselves to talk. She said she'd see me for dinner, and I drove back out to the cabin, thought about trying the boat and the fishing gear and decided I didn't know enough about them and had better wait for Kit to show me. I had a beer from Kit's refrigerator and went to sleep out on the sun deck. By the time I had awakened, had another beer, and showered and dressed, it was dinner time. I drove back to Catherton and to Ma's. She had another steak for me, and she again closed the café so that we were alone.

"You goin' back out to Annie's tonight," she said.

"Kit tell you?"

"Didn't have to. I know 'im. He don't hunt fights, but he never run from one, neither." She leaned back against the soft-drink cooler. "You ever see a old boar coon? One

79

that's run half the night before the dogs caught up to 'im, that has swum cricks and climbed trees to cross over to other trees before he come down and run again, and did ever' damn thing that had got 'im away before. This night none of it worked, so the dogs are down there under 'im, and you come up with a lantern and start choppin' down the tree."

"No, Ma, I've never been coon hunting."

"Need to go. Can learn a lot from a coon like that."

"How? What could I learn?"

She straightened, leaned toward me, made sure of what she was going to say. "It'd be better if you'd seen it. The coon's done ever'thing he knows and he's caught. Now a coon's smart, smarter'n a man in a lot of ways, so he knows the hounds will kill 'im when the tree goes down. The thing is, he ain't scared or sorry. He sits there and watches you chop, interested in it like he was outside of it, had paid for a safe seat for hisself, and, when the tree's down, he don't try to run, but he don't quit. He fights the best he can. He knows he's through once and for all, but he ain't scared, just interested in fightin', in showin' how good he can prove out against a dozen or two dozen hounds, all of 'em bigger'n he is." She stopped talking and looked off into nothing, then shook her big head, and fastened her eyes on me. "Kit's like that coon, Jud," she said. "He has decided he won't wait for the tree choppin'. He has come down to fight."

"Fight what, Ma?"

"Don't play fact-hidin' games with me, boy. First he'll close up Annie." She snorted. "A sixteen-year-old girl out there. Then he'll take on the big hounds, the whole pack of 'em, up north."

"Who owns those hounds?" I asked.

"I'm a old country woman," she said, "but I listen good. There has been men in from Joplin up to Lake City;

they ain't there for any good. They ain't there for the fishin'. Got me a friend up there runs a eatin' place. She says they come in ever' week or two, make the rounds of them sin holes, wear ties, talk nice but walk mean."

"You think organized crime has moved in?"

"Hell, I know the word. Syndicate. Kit wouldn't listen to me six months ago, so I shut up about it. I don't need to draw it out for you, Jud. You stay near 'im. You mind?"

"I mind, Ma."

The billing had changed at the movie. I saw a spy picture that wasn't meant to be funny but was, extremely. Fred was back at the desk when I got to the City–County building. "Kit's home sleepin'," he said. "Will be in after bit. I guess you're goin' out there with 'im again tonight."

"I guess," I said.

"Hell, you don't guess; you know," he said. "Said I couldn't go along, got to stay here. Well, by God, another day or two and I'll have somethin' to show 'im."

"What, Fred?" He sounded definite, proud of himself.

"I aim to be sure first, but I figger I will be," he said.

He wouldn't talk more about it. I read a cattleman's magazine, smoked, drank coffee, and waited until Kit came in. He looked rested. At two in the morning we drove to Annie's. "Just watch my back," he said. "Otis is dumb enough to git mean."

We both went to the door. Kit knocked. Otis opened the door the length of the lock chain and then started to close it hurriedly. The door bounced off his shoulder as Kit drove hard into it with his shoulder, snapping the chain and exploding into the room. He switched on the lights Annie had turned on the night before and the room froze into a static tableau. One of the girls who had been there the night before had been dancing with a youngster, no more than eighteen or nineteen, and they stopped in the middle of a step; he even had one foot clear of the floor.

81

A man in one of the booths stopped his drink halfway up—or down—from his mouth. Annie sat—was puddled would be better—in the booth at the end of the room, her head down on her arms, a two-thirds-empty quart bottle in front of her. Kit didn't hesitate; he started for the door at the back of the room, and Otis, recovering from the door's slam into him, started after him, sliding a little in his hurry, gathering an empty beer bottle off the bar as he went. I had started when Otis did, and I hit him across the back and the side of his neck with the edge of my hand. I'm no karate man, but I know the basics, and Otis kept sliding on down to the floor. Kit didn't even look back. He opened the door and went in, and I saw that Otis was no longer interested in anything and went to the door behind Kit.

Four men scrabbled to their feet from around a circular table that held cards and chips. A fifth man stayed in his seat. The four looked for a way out and I blocked the door. The seated man looked at Kit and smiled, the smile of no surprise, no matter what, the smile of a professional. "Gentlemen," he said, "I call this game closed."

"For good," Kit said.

"For good is a long time," the man at the table said.

"You takin' us in, Kit, just for settin' in on a friendly game?" one of the four asked.

"Git outta here, Clarence," Kit said. "I ain't interested in none of you." I stepped away from the door and they left the room as fast as Kit had come into it.

"I don't know you," Kit said to the fifth man, "and I don't plan to git to know you, because you have run your last game in my county."

"Possibly," the man said. He had a thin, expressionless face, looked like a neat clerk in a men's store, but he was no clerk; too much lay behind that lack of expression. "Are you taking me in, sheriff?"

"No. I'd rather you stayed out to spread the word," Kit said.

"It will be spread." He smiled; his eyes didn't. He got up from the table, didn't bother to touch cards or chips, and left.

Kit put both hands under the edge of the table and heaved. It crashed over onto its top, turning over two of the chairs around it. "Always wanted to try that," Kit said to me. "Like a real western sheriff. It's satisfyin'."

Otis recovered enough to walk to our car. Kit and I had to carry Annie between us, her feet dragging on the gravel.

EIGHT

I woke up at seven-thirty after three hours' sleep, and fall, or the foretaste of it, had come; light but steady rain, pushed by fitful wind, streamed down the tall sun deck windows, glistened the green tree leaves, and turned the lake into gray slate. Kit had said there was no reason to come in until afternoon or night, so I pulled the Indian blanket up to my chin, congratulated myself on how comfortable I was and let the rain put me back to sleep. I didn't get up until noon. I made and drank coffee, took a long, hot shower, then a cool one, and called Kit's office. This was Saturday, and I'd gotten here Thursday, and this was the first time I had used the phone. Neither had it rung. That's the way a phone should be treated, used about once every three or four days; too often a phone uses you. I found myself deciding I could use a lot of this Oklahoma life, right here in this cabin on this lake. Frank answered.

"Kit there?" I asked.

"Who is this?"

"Jud Blade."

"Sure. Just a second."

"Mornin', Jud," Kit said. "You just git up?"

"Little bit ago. How's Annie?"

"Hung over. When she gits over it, she is gonna kill me and maybe you. Said so in about two thousand words, half cussin'."

"Did you arraign her?"

"Three hours ago," Kit said. "Out on bond again."

"How's Otis?"

"Got him a hell of a sore neck. He's out, too."

"How about Tug Wilson?"

"I'm holdin' 'im. Me and Mercer and James talked it over with Billy Joe awhile ago, and we decided to hold 'im on suspicion while we look around some more. Mercer don't like it, but he went along."

"How long can you hold him?" I asked. I sat down on one of the bar stools and watched a bluejay hop under a tree, strutting even with wet feathers.

"Seventy-two hours. Swimmer is the onliest one liable to git particular about it."

"What's on for today and tonight?"

"Depends," Kit said. "We may have to go back out to Annie's, but I will guess we'll go up north on the lake, git into a little larger league." Ma had been right.

"Any hurry about my coming in?"

"Nary'n. Ain't much of a day for fishin' though," Kit said. The rural connection was a little scratchy and I could hear wire noise that sounded like lonesome, far-away wind.

"How about dinner at Ma's?"

"See you there about seven."

"I'll be there," I said. Kit hung up, and I put the phone back, turned on the television set and watched the noon news while I made a sandwich out of sliced ham I found in the refrigerator. It went well with beer.

I didn't hear a car drive up or stop outside, probably because it made no sound on the bare, wet ground and because no one closed a door when he got out. I heard the bluejay scream, but I didn't know how good a watchdog a bluejay can be. I was lying on the couch, studying the ceiling and the too few facts I had gathered, wondering how long it would take for Kit's tactics to touch off reaction and speculating on what that reaction would be, when I felt the sudden sureness that I wasn't by myself. They burst in through the sun deck door while I swung my feet off the couch and stood beside it. Two men came in first; Annie stood behind them, short and shapeless, her gray-green eyes slitted and mean. "That's him. That's the Yankee, writer sonofabitch," she said. "I told you we'd find 'im out here at Marlow's place."

"Sit down," one of the men told me. He was the older of the two, probably in his late twenties, about as big as I, well dressed, coat and tie; his big, dark face had features that were too small and he would need to shave at least twice a day. The other looked about twenty, long hair combed carefully, wide, loose mouth; his coat hung too large on him and he kept his right hand just inside the left lapel, stereotype of a punk with a gun.

"Social call?" I said. I had changed clothes after showering and hadn't yet transferred my gun to my pants pocket, but I had taped my knife on when I had dressed. I didn't sit.

"Maybe," he said. "It's up to you."

"Maybe, hell," Annie said. "He busted Otis. I want the shit kicked outta him."

"Shut up," the older man told her. "It's this way, Blade: You aren't law. You're a lousy-assed writer sucking up for a story, but you're a good friend of Marlow's. He talks to you, has been talking to you for two days. What does he talk about?" His accent sounded midwestern but it definitely wasn't Oklahoman. He didn't drop a "g."

"About closing Annie down," I said.

"Why? Why all of a sudden? Alexander had told her she could operate. Briggs will see it the same way."

"She had a sixteen-year-old girl out there," I said. "That made Kit mad." I decided to answer enough questions with enough sense to draw more questions. Sometimes I learn as much from questions as I do from answers.

"I explained that, Paul," Annie said hurriedly. "Git on with what we come out here for."

"I told you to shut up and I told you not to use my name," he said. That had irritated him. "We got more time than you got sense. All right, Blade, who's next?"

"What do you mean next?"

"Is Marlow going to stop with Annie or is he going to keep it up?" He sat down on one of the couches.

"Like you said, I'm a lousy-assed writer. I don't make Kit's plans for him. I just go along for the story," I said.

"Let me have 'im," the younger one said.

"Wait," the older one said. "You've been around enough and long enough to know this isn't for fun, Blade. Answer me."

"I did."

"I didn't like the way you did." He got up, walked to me, and slapped me, not too hard. Then, with easy, calculated precision, he slapped me three times more, waiting to let each blow have its effect. I took it, not allowing anger to start. This was not the time to tip whatever hand I held.

"Lay it on the sonofabitch," Annie screeched. "Don't play with 'im."

"Now," the man said. "Who is next?"

"He said we might go up north on the lake tonight," I said. I tried to let a quiver into my voice.

"What place?"

"He didn't say."

He slapped me twice again, a little harder, enough to jar me. "What place?" This was a job to him. He seemed to be fair at it, but he wasn't one of the kind who really enjoy it.

"He still didn't say, so I still don't know," I said.

He hit me in the belly, a good, controlled hook, and I took that, too. He thought about the punch before he threw it and I had time to harden my stomach muscles. I thought it was time to let him think he'd hurt me. He had, as a matter of fact, but not seriously. I sat down on the couch and bent to a pain cramp I didn't have.

"I can do this all day," he said.

"Bust eight or ten ribs and he'll by God tell you," Annie said. She went over to rummage in the service bar, came up with a quart of Jack Daniel's, uncapped it, poured out a water tumbler half full, and drank it. She didn't need chaser.

"I don't know," I said.

"Stand up," he said, and I did. He hit me again in the same place, quite a lot harder. It hurt quite a lot more.

"Please," I grunted. "I don't know."

"Let me take the bastard," the younger one said. He took his right hand down from his coat lapel, put it into his right pants pocket, came out with a knife and pushed the button. The long, thin blade shot into place.

"Let 'im have 'im," Annie yelled like a cheerleader. She poured herself another drink of Kit's good whisky. "Cut a ear off."

Knives scare me. I know what I can do with mine. I decided the older one, the one in front of me, would keep asking the same question, and I didn't have an answer, and that sooner or later he'd let the young one with the knife have me—or try to have me—and I'd been cowed and easy long enough.

The one in front of me started another hook, wide and careless, the kind of a punch you throw at the heavy bag because you know it can't hit back. I caught his arm and made a basic throw, turning my body down as I spun him over. I brought his arm sharply over my tensed knee at the finish. Two or three things tore and snapped; I heard them clearly in the sudden silence. He squealed once, then hit the floor hard with the side of his head and lay quiet. I came up to a quick crouch, located the younger one, who was busy realizing that he was now on his own. When he did, he tried, but that's about all I can say for him.

"All right, you bastard," he said. "Now you git it; now you git it all." He started toward me.

I could have done it a little easier by throwing my knife, but, for me to be sure while he was moving, I might have had to kill him. I had nothing against that except that it might complicate things for both me and Kit, so I reached back and drew my knife but held it. He stopped as if he had run into a wall. This tore his script. When he had a knife and started for someone, that someone begged or ran; he didn't come up from nowhere with a knife of his own. But his was longer than mine and his punk's pride stood at stake and he recovered and came on, fast. He held his knife in fair position, in front of him but a little wide and high. He had forgotten his gun. If he had remembered, I would have thrown.

I stepped inside his sweeping thrust, clamped down hard on his knife wrist with my left hand, and made one deep, neat cut. His knife clattered when it hit the wooden floor. I tossed mine to the couch to free my right hand, took his gun, a .38 with a barrel too long to fit well into his shoulder holster, then dropped his arm. He grabbed his wrist with his left hand and blood poured through his fingers. "Oh, my God," he said. He turned greenish white.

I checked Annie. She stood stupidly at the bar, her mouth half open and her eyes unbelieving. I waved the gun at her. "Come over here," I said. "You know how to tie a tourniquet?"

Tough women react better than all but the toughest men, and Annie had no gentleness left in her, if there had ever been any. She put down her glass, waddled across to us. She took the punk's handkerchief out of the breast pocket of his coat, wadded it and stuck it over the slash on his wrist. With her other hand she unbuckled his belt and slipped it out, cinched it hard around the knot of the handkerchief, and held it there.

The one on the floor stirred, groaned and sat up after two tries. I took his gun from his coat, a short-barreled, efficient .38. He finally made it to his feet, pulling at the couch with his left arm. His broken right arm hung crooked and useless.

"Can you drive, Annie?" I said. "You better get to a doctor. Your friends are going to be one-handed for a good long time, maybe forever for that one you've got there."

"You mother-raping son of a bitch," she said. None of it had frightened her. She put the end of the belt in the man's left hand. "Hold your own god-damned bandage."

The other one could talk through his pain. "Next time," he said. "Next time."

She herded them through the door, down the steps, and into the back seat of the car, a black Ford with Missouri license tags. She got in behind the wheel and spun tires on the slickening clay and gravel as she left.

I got a pan of cold water and a couple of towels, cleaned

up the blood; there was quite a bit of it. I wondered if he'd get to a doctor in time. I called Kit and told him what had happened. He didn't ask if I was all right, and I took that as a compliment.

"How come you and not me?" he asked.

"You're law. They stay away from that as long as they can. And I looked easy all alone out here," I said.

"How come you didn't shoot the bastards?"

"No real need." I didn't tell him I had been careless about the gun. I wouldn't be again.

"Maybe you better move outta there," he said.

"I like it here."

"But you turnin' into the bait," he said. "You want me to have 'em picked up? They got to git to a doctor; they oughtta be fairly easy for me to find."

"No need," I said. "Those two won't be coming back."

"Missouri tags, you say?"

"I say. What's the syndicate geography up north, Kit?"

He thought about it awhile. "I ain't a authority on it. FBI man comes in here tells me they strong in Kansas City, got a branch operation in Joplin, and a man can gamble as easy in that town as he can in Las Vegas, so he is prob'ly right."

"You realize what we're going up against, Kit?"

"I aim to push, Jud." I thought about Ma's boar coon story. "You comin' in now?"

"Later, Kit." We hung up.

We met at Ma's a little after seven, and I told the story of the afternoon again for her and for Kit.

"Maybe you'd ruther have your steak raw?" she said. "I hear tigers eat 'em that way."

"Annie has flew her coop," Kit said. "She must have kept on goin' with them two. I drove out by there awhile ago, and the place is boarded up. Then I found one of them girls she had out there, workin' over to the Palace

Grill now, and she told me Annie and Otis packed up and boarded up late this mornin'. Annie told this girl it'd be awhile 'fore she comes back, but said she was comin'."

"Damn good riddance," Ma said. "But she was the easy, close-to-hand one, old man; she wasn't one of the big ones."

"What do you know about it, old woman?"

" 'Nough to know you'll be goin' up north tonight," she said.

"How come you know that?"

"Where does a goose go when it gits cold?"

"South," Kit said.

"That's how come you're goin' north. A goose has got good sense."

"You don't make none," he said.

"Those people will be waitin' for you now," she said.

"I'll oblige 'em."

"And it is liable to be the death of you. Them two with Jud meant business, even if they was the ones got the business. You know and I know it can git a lot meaner. You goin' along tonight, Jud?"

"I wouldn't miss it," I said.

"Good."

"When and how come did you take to worryin' 'bout me, old woman?" Kit said.

"Who else would? That's enough talk. Eat." She served the steaks.

When we left, Kit stopped at the door and said, "Fine dinner, Charity." It was the first time I had heard her name.

"No need to soft-soap me," she said.

"Don't worry," he said. "I'll see you for breakfast." His voice was gentle with her.

We drove to the office in separate cars. Frank was at the desk. "Where's Fred?" Kit asked.

"Called in and asked me if it'd be all right if he came in late. Said he was hot on somethin'," Frank said. "He's bccn ovei aiuuiid the courthouse today askin' questions. Bessie told me."

"Detectin', most likely," Kit said. "More power to 'im."

We were going to the Paradise Club on Grand Lake, Kit told me when we were seated in his office, more to talk to the owner than to raid, because the owner, Jack Simmons, was the head of an informal but rigid association of club and bar owners in the county. "Like I told you before, he's the one brought Ben 'is money ever' month," Kit said. "I'd like to know who all furnished the money."

"You don't think he'll ever tell you, do you, Kit?"

" 'Course not, but he will git the message I will be carryin': that I'm shuttin' things down. And when Jack gits it, ever'body gits it."

We killed time around the office until ten-thirty, then drove the winding twenty miles north to the resort town of Lake City. Two cafés, a bait shop, a drugstore, a VFW hall, two service stations, a couple of beer halls and three nightclubs, private clubs under Oklahoma law, made up the whole town. Kit parked his car at the largest of the clubs, a long, wide, cement-block building with an abbreviated, laced-canvas canopy and a large, red neon sign that blinked on and off: *PARADISE.*

"Now I doubt that there is any use," Kit said, "but you go on in first like we done at Annie's and see if'n you can order a drink. We might as well let Jack know we are givin' it the old college try."

No chain held the door; the place was wide open. A Saturday night crowd pretty well filled the big room and its booths; fifteen or twenty couples danced; the long, polished bar, lighted softly and tastefully, was popular but not crowded. A bartender in a white mess jacket, clean and starched, said, "Yes?"

"Bourbon and water. Make it a double; it's a warm night."

"Are you a member, sir, and what's your bottle number?" he said.

"I'm a tourist, just passing through," I said.

"I'm terribly sorry, sir, but this is a private club. You have to be a member." He couldn't manage to keep back his grin, and it told me I would be wasting any further acting, if what I had done could be called acting.

"Word does get around in Oklahoma, doesn't it?" I said.

"Does for a fact, Mr. Blade," he said.

Kit came in and took the stool beside me. "Hi, Harold," he said to the bartender.

"Evenin', Kit."

"Nice crowd."

"You know Saturdays."

"Slot machines put away, Harold?"

"What machines, Kit?"

"Back room closed?"

"The storage room's padlocked, Kit."

"I bet that hurts old Jack. Sattiday night with the machines moved out and the storage room locked. Where is he?"

"Jack's in his office," the bartender said. He couldn't have been more pleasant.

"I'll just go on in. All right if this here tourist next to me goes along? It don't look like he is gonna be able to git a Sattiday night buzz on."

"I'm sure he'll be welcome," the bartender said. "As welcome as you are, Kit."

"I bet," Kit said. He got down off the stool. "Come on, Jud."

We went to the far end of the bar and Kit knocked on a door in the side wall of the room. "Come in," somebody said. We did. The office looked like that of a Chicago executive: carpet, soft occasional chairs, a bleached-mahogany desk, stereo-television set against one wall, soft lighting. The man behind the desk seemed out of place. He wore a white knit shirt, open at the neck, had the shoulders of a good, brawling welterweight and the face of a fighter who never could or would cover up from punishment. Both eyebrows glistened with scar tissue; his nose had been broken and rebroken and apparently never set; white scar line showed through the stubble of his salt-and-pepper hair; one ear was misshapen. His voice surprised me, modulated but distinct, careful in articulation. "Good evening, Kit," he said. "Hello, Mr. Blade."

"Hi, Jack," Kit said. "Always tickles me to git to say that. Almost as good as 'Hi, Gene.'"

"Tickles a lot of people." He came around the desk and shook hands with Kit, then with me. We sat down. "If you really want that drink, Mr. Blade, I'd be pleased to pour you one. No charge. It's legal in here."

"I'd be pleased to take it," I said.

"Kit?" Simmons asked.

"Believe not, bein' as how I'm anyway halfway on duty."

"If I remember right, it's bourbon and water," Simmons said to me.

"You don't remember, but you heard," I said. An impressive intercom sat on his desk; there would be a receiver behind the bar. He mixed from a bar behind his desk, gave me the glass. "Thank you, Mr. Simmons."

"Call me Jack, please."

"I will. You call me Jud." I tasted the drink; fine bourbon.

"That takes care of the social end of it," Kit said. "Jack, you gonna lose money tonight, machines gone, back room closed, nothin' but setups over the bar." He didn't sound

95

or look gleeful about it; he sounded more as if he were reproaching Simmons.

"I'll manage, Kit," Simmons said, "but it's good of you to worry about it."

"But then you savin' on your monthly payments," Kit said.

"I'm sorry we are," Simmons said. He lighted a cigarette with a small-sized gold lighter. "Maybe it won't have to stay that way."

"I aim to see it does," Kit said.

"For a fact?"

"You can write 'er down, Jack."

"I just did."

These two obviously knew each other well. No personal enmity, no rancor; respect both ways, and, as far as I could tell, honesty. Their familiarity let them talk in shorthand. I managed to follow.

"I liked Ben," Kit said.

"I did, too," Simmons said. "You've got Tug. That's a good thing for you."

"No."

"You can make it a good thing."

"Not good enough," Kit said. "Got to be true to be good enough."

"Truth a lot of times comes hard," Simmons said.

"Not too hard," Kit said. "If a man is willin' to pay for it." He had leaned forward in his chair while he talked; now he leaned back.

"A man can't pay if he hasn't got the money," Simmons said.

"A man can borrow; money, marbles, chalk, even a name," Kit said.

"I would borrow if I could. I can't."

"Then that's it. We'll see you, Jack."

I put my glass down on the glass-topped table next to

96

my chair, thanked Simmons for it, and followed Kit out of the office, out of the club. He drove several miles before he said, "You followed 'im, didn't you, Jud?"

"Yes."

"Either he don't know, which is possible, or he can't afford to let hisself know, which is mighty possible. I know one thing: Jack ain't hisself, ain't the way he used to be. Something or somebody has changed 'im."

We got back to Catherton about midnight. Kit drove out past Annie's to check, and the place huddled in dark melancholy. He toured the highway north and south, the road east and west, finally turned down the side street and parked in front of his office. We got out and went up the walk, and he opened the door. I followed him in. "Fred must be in back," he said before we went around the end of the counter. "No," he said. "Oh, Christ, no."

Fred lay on his back, behind and to the side of his desk. His head almost touched a bank of file cabinets. One foot in its cowboy boot extended under the corner leg of his desk; the other leg pointed straight out at Kit and me. Fred had no right eye, only a bullet-smashed hole. Blood and brain tissue splotched the front of one file cabinet, and, from the look of the floor, I knew that Fred no longer had much, if any, back to his head.

NINE

Neither Kit nor I moved for dragging seconds. It was obscenely and bloodily obvious we could do nothing for Fred. I looked at Kit, white under his tan, and saw that he had begun to do the next thing to do: study the room. I joined him. The fluorescent lights, strung into the ceiling without softening baffles under them, seemed to have gained in intensity, throwing down harsh light that magnified detail.

Blood and brain matter on the five-drawer file cabinet behind Fred's desk and chair were at the height of a seated man's head. Fred had been shot while sitting behind his desk.

The chair, a straight one that Fred had liked to tilt on its back legs, lay two feet to the left of the body. The impact of the bullet and the convulsive jerk of Fred's dying had knocked it down with him. A compact tape recorder that I hadn't seen before sat on top the desk, one spool gone, the other empty. Except for the body, the splotched file cabinet, the chair and the recorder, nothing in the room had changed, not in any aspect that I could determine.

Kit moved first. He stepped around the end of the desk, over Fred's pointing leg, opened the top right-hand drawer of the desk, took out a long-barreled .38, checked the cylinder and put the gun back in the drawer. "No chance to git to it," he said. He turned suddenly, stepped back over the leg and walked down the hall toward the far end of the building. He came back in less than a minute. "Tug's gone," he said. "Cell door's wide open. Fred's keys are still in the door."

"Other prisoners?" I asked.

"Just Tug. Had him in a security cell; rest are in the tank at the back. They all asleep."

"A gun would have made a big noise in here."

"Fire wall and a steel door between here and there. Hard to hear anything. Could have been a silencer."

"Could have been," I said. "One thing. I've never seen the recorder. Does it belong here?"

"No, but I've seen it, or Ben had one just like it. It's been over there in the office. You see anything else?"

"No."

"Me, neither." He looked again at the body, not flinching, no longer white except around his mouth. "Fred was a good man, a damn good man, my friend. Been with me a long time."

"You said Tug has a son."

"He does, a wild one, and about a hundred other kinfolks, most all of 'em wild, some of 'em mean."

"Mean enough for this?"

"If Fred tried to stop 'em, which he would, but it don't look like he'd have stayed in the chair if he saw one of 'em come in." He picked up the phone and dialed a number. "Might as well git to it." I could hear the thin,

99

intermittent buzz as the phone rang. "James?" Kit said. "You and Mercer better git down here to the office. No, now. Fred's been killed." He listened briefly. "He's gone. What? I remember you did. Maybe you was right. Prob'ly you was. No. Just the way we found it. Blade and me. All right." He hung up. "They'll be right down," he told me. "Let's go to my office a minute." He opened the desk drawer, and both he and I took long drinks from his unlabeled bottle. He used his phone there to call Frank and ask him to come down. We went back to the outer office. "Fred was seventy-one last week. Wouldn't't've thought it, would you, Jud?"

"No, I wouldn't."

"Lawed all 'is life. I should've taken two drinks."

Mercer and James came in, coats but no ties. James was combing his hair. They were professionals and they took it all in quickly. Mercer kneeled by the body, touched the back of his hand to Fred's throat, flexed an inert arm at the elbow. "How long since you found him?" he asked.

"Maybe fifteen minutes," Kit said. "No longer'n that."

"Hasn't been dead much more than an hour," Mercer said. I doubted that he could be accurate. It was warm in the room. His touch wasn't that sensitive.

"Shot him out of the chair," James said. "He was dead before he hit the floor."

"And Wilson's gone," Mercer said. I heard possible self-satisfaction in his voice.

"He's gone," Kit said.

"He was your responsibility," Mercer said.

"He was," Kit said. "So's this."

Mercer should have eased up. Lawmen, even if they don't admire or respect each other's tactics or abilities, usually recognize kinship, especially when it's hard-shared. He didn't. "You left an old man to do a young man's job," he said. "Where were you?"

100

Kit looked at Mercer, opened his mouth to answer, then closed it and swallowed hard. "Up north," he said. "Tryin' to do my job. We found Fred when we got back. Called you at the motel a minute or two later." I could see the effort he was making to hold his temper, to work with Mercer.

Butler came in, looked carefully at the body and then away at the wall, back at the body. He clapped his hand to his mouth and turned and ran down the hall.

"He's thinking it could have been him," James said. "I felt the same way and thought the same thing on my first one."

"He's still new at this," Kit said.

"Where did the recorder come from?" Mercer asked. "It wasn't here earlier." His darting, shifting black eyes missed nothing.

"One like it's been in Ben's office, was his," Kit said. "Fred must've borried it."

"Why?"

"I got no idea."

James prowled behind the desk and around the body, pointed to a dent in the spattered, dull-green file cabinet, began to scan the floor along the wall and back to the corner it made with the front counter.

"Bullet hit there?" Kit asked. He and I should have seen it. We hadn't.

"Looks that way. Must have gone on through his head," James said. "Ought to be here."

We all four began to look. Kit found it tucked partially under Fred's left shoulder, almost hidden, straightened with it in his palm. The front of it had flattened, exploded until its raggedness was nearly the diameter of a quarter.

"Must have been hollow-point," Mercer said. He took it from Kit's hand. "Probably .38."

"Lab will know," James said. He held out his hand and Mercer gave him the bullet.

Frank came back into the room, white and shaken but in control. "You want pictures?" he asked.

"Guess you'd better," Kit said. Frank got a four-by-five Graphic and its attachments from a cabinet at the back of the room, and we backed away from the body while he took flash pictures from four angles. Kit got a plastic bag for the bullet, and James wrapped it, put it in his coat pocket.

"We all through?" Kit asked.

"All except getting Wilson and whoever took him out of here," Mercer said. "Probably the son. When we get them we'll be all through."

Kit picked up the phone and called for an ambulance. "Hate to let Fred lay there any longer'n I have to," he said. "Will you want an autopsy?"

"No need," Mercer said. "We've already got the bullet."

After the ambulance had come and the attendants had wrapped Fred's body and taken it away, the four of us, Mercer, James, Kit and I, sat in Kit's office. "You'll want to get an all-points bulletin out on Wilson," Mercer said.

"We damn near all the points I got," Kit said. "One other deputy, Monroe, works the south end of the county. Him and Frank and me and the day jailer are it now."

"We'll get more men in," James said. "You got any idea where Wilson'll be?"

"Know where he'll be," Kit said.

"Then we'll go after him first thing in the morning," Mercer said. "I'll guess we'll have to bring him in dead." He grinned his grin that wasn't one. "I hope we have to bring him in dead."

"You remember back in the thirties when Pretty Boy Floyd and a lot of other hard ones hung out in the hills north and east of here?" Kit asked.

"Remember hearing about it," Mercer said.

"Governor decided to clean out them hills," Kit said, "so he called out a bunch of National Guard and lawmen from all around here. I wasn't in on it, but I been told about it. Them soldiers and the lawmen didn't have sense enough to git 'em a good tree and set under it; they fought them rocks, trees, and hills for three days and some of three nights. Half of 'em got lost, and the rest of 'em had to hunt those. They all got wore clear out, and two, three busted legs fallin' off cliffs. They tore up Model A's and army trucks. If they'd had tanks, they'd've torn 'em up, too. When it was all over, they had caught three moonshiners who had got fallin' down drunk at their own still and couldn't run and a couple cow thieves that had come in from the outside and didn't know the country. Old Tug knows them hills like you and me know our livin' rooms, maybe better."

"That's where he is?" Mercer asked.

"That's where," Kit said. "And you right. You ever find 'im, you'll have to drag 'im outta there dead. But you ain't likely to find 'im." He didn't have doubt in his voice.

"This is nineteen seventy," James said, "not back in the thirties."

"Them hills don't count time," Kit said. "Places back in there it is still about eighteen hundred and ten."

"We'll get the dogs from McAlester," Mercer said.

"I ain't knockin' them dogs, but Tug is a hell of a lot smarter'n a possum," Kit said. "We talkin' 'bout two, three thousand square miles. We won't know where Tug went in."

"Somebody will know," James said. "And, like always, somebody will tell." He sounded very sure of his maxim.

"No," Kit said.

"What do you mean no?" Mercer said.

"I mean somebody ain't about to tell. I know them people."

"There has to be a way," James said. "Good God, this is nineteen hundred and seventy."

"You already said that," Kit said. "There's a way, maybe: Swimmer."

"Who's Swimmer?" Mercer asked.

"Indian friend of mine and Tug's lawyer," Kit said. "We'll talk to 'im in the mornin'."

"And he—this Indian—can do something? By himself?" Mercer asked.

"If it can git done," Kit said.

"If it gets done, we'll have to do it," Mercer said. "I don't trust any damned Indian. Keep him out of it."

"Listen," Kit said, "you been in the city too long. There's things . . ." He held himself again. "It's past three. Can we do anything else tonight?"

"I guess not," Mercer said. "Don and I will call the bureau from the motel. We'll see you here about eight."

"I'll be here," Kit said.

"Bigger story than you expected to run into, Mr. Blade," James said.

Mercer paid attention to me for the first time that night. "How come you were along with Marlow tonight?" he asked.

"I asked 'im," Kit said.

"I told you I don't approve of the press working with the law."

"I told you it's my county," Kit said.

"Maybe not for long," Mercer said.

"Kit and I walked in cold on this tonight," I said. "He couldn't very well run me off after we did."

"I guess he couldn't. I could have," Mercer said. "Let's go, Don." They left.

Kit stood at the window and watched their car lights pull away from the curb and turn up the street. He turned back to his desk and got out his bottle for the second time. "You, Jud?"

"No thanks, Kit."

He took a short one, put the bottle away. "You sleepy?"

"No."

"Let's go up to Fred's house."

"Does he—did he—have a wife?"

"Wife's dead. Got two kids down in Texas. I'll call 'em in the mornin'. Lived by hisself."

Frank had used soap, water, a mop, and jail disinfectant. The floor still shone wetly, and he still looked sick. Kit asked him if he would be all right there alone, and he said he would try to be. He didn't sound sure about it. We got in Kit's car and drove north eight or ten blocks to the edge of town, stopped at a small frame house, opened the unlocked door and turned on the lights. There were four rooms, living room, bedroom, kitchen, bath, all sparsely, spartanly furnished, bare and cheerless. It reminded me of army bachelors' office quarters.

"What will we look for?" I asked Kit.

"I don't rightly know, Jud. Maybe tapes."

"For that recorder on the desk?"

"A man don't borry a recorder unless he's got somethin' to record or listen to. You look around the livin' room and the kitchen. I'll take the bedroom and the bathroom."

We spent thirty minutes in the house and we found no tapes, nothing that we couldn't have expected to find. Some men leave little physical mark to represent years, even seventy of them, and Fred had been such a man. I had found keys at a desk in the living room, and Kit locked the house behind us after he turned out the lights. We parked at the curb at the City-County building. "You may as well go on back out and git some sleep," Kit said.

"Would it be better if I didn't come in in the morning?" I knew it would be.

"Maybe so," Kit said. "I am gonna be up past my neck in people, includin' the newspaper and tee vee boys from Tulsa, who wouldn't take too kindly to you bein' in on this from the beginnin' and who don't need to know you in on it at all. Besides, they ain't gonna be nothin' done tomorry. I'll call you. Maybe you and me and Swimmer can talk after things clear out."

I stopped at the door on my way out. "Will you quit pushing now, Kit, up north? The ones Annie brought after me today—yesterday—were second rate. If they send someone after you, and that's liable to be next, he'll rate higher, maybe high enough. And it looks as if Mercer's right, that Wilson did it."

"He didn't do this tonight," Kit said. "Fred kept them jail keys on his belt nights. Somebody else shot 'im, took 'em, and let Tug out."

"You said Wilson's son or some of his other kin would do it."

"Not when they could just as easy have banged Fred in the head a little and let Tug out, not when they could've manhandled Fred back there and left 'im in Tug's place, which is what they would've done, because then they'd be a joke to it. Nobody had to shoot Fred in a hurry. He hadn't even opened that drawer with 'is gun in it."

"Then you still don't think Wilson killed Ben and Ben's girl?"

"I've tried to hoe that row, Jud; am still tryin', and it's like one man choppin' cotton in a bottom-land section; I just don't never git to the logical end of it."

"You didn't answer me about the pushing," I said.

"You're gittin' as bad as Ma Maxwell for worryin'. I

aim to keep on. I let that go too long and I ain't proud I did."

"As long as you've got people, Kit, here or anywhere, you're going to have drinking and gambling."

"Sure. I am all in favor of havin' 'em." He grinned at me with a tired mouth. "Country style. No more sixteen-year-old gals in places like Annie's. No more poker dealers like the one we run into out there, because it is hard enough to win a dollar in a honest game. No matter what the preachers say, a man can compromise with sin. Hell, this business, you got to."

"It takes two sides to compromise," I said.

"We'll see. I'll call out to the cabin, prob'ly in the afternoon."

"I'll see you tomorrow."

I had a lot to think about on my way to the cabin, but my brain had gone a lot of miles since morning and it ground away slowly. A lot of times I get leap transference —going from a single primary, even secondary thought to a complete, valid conclusion without need for intermediate steps. Not tonight. Was the syndicate, the Mafia, the Cosa Nostra in control? Did someone push an organization button to send Annie and the two men after me, or did Annie hire the two on her own hook? No, she didn't because they had come to find out how much further Kit would go, was going to go, what would happen up north. Those two weren't working for Annie. They weren't working at all right now—and wouldn't be for awhile. I felt satisfaction in that, because my stomach had turned sore from the punches.

Kit, at first believing, ostensibly, that someone local had killed Alexander and his fiancée, killed them for revenge and out of hate for Alexander, had then switched and taken an iron lock on the theory, my theory, that the killings had been professional. He didn't believe Wilson was guilty. All right, that makes a peculiar sort of sense: Kit felt guilty because he hadn't stopped whatever organized crime there was earlier, because things had gotten out of hand, out of his hands. He'd naturally feel some sort of relief that someone from his county, someone he knew, probably liked, hadn't done it. He seemed to like Wilson. Why not? Maybe Wilson is likeable. If guts are a criterion for making a man likeable, he probably is, because if Butler had taken the cuffs off him in the outer office, he would have gone after Mercer, sap or not. Are guts of that kind also a criterion for a murder and a rape? That depends on definition of guts. I doubt that they are.

Kit had said he would keep on pushing, at least until he dictated a compromise. Jack Simmons had seemed like a man who would compromise, but the syndicate would not, not for one county sheriff. Kit is being naive there. They might sit back, wait, and elect themselves another sheriff, one with his hand out, his back turned and his eyes closed. If it is syndicate, Kit would be lucky if they took that route.

Wouldn't I be lucky, too? I came down here to find and punish, one way or another, a rapist-killer. That's the reason I travel, the aim I have in life. Not all true: I came down here to help Kit, because he asked me.

Did I bargain to help take on the syndicate? No, I didn't bargain. I told Kit and Ma Maxwell I would. So, if necessary, I will, but with open eyes, because the syndicate would have far less compunction, realistic compunction, not moral, about erasing or crippling me than they would have about Kit.

I drove over the hill crest on the approach road and saw a light in the cabin. I turned off my car lights and my engine and coasted to a stop short of the cul-de-sac. A pickup truck was parked under one of the big elms. Syndicate people don't drive pickups or wait with lights on, I told myself, but I put my hand in my pocket, pushed the spring, and flipped off the safety on my gun as I checked out the truck. It was empty. I went up the steps to the sun deck cautiously, kept out of the light that reached through the door and windows. Swimmer sat in one of the big leather chairs, his back partially toward me, his feet up on the oak table. I let out my breath and opened the door.

"Come on in and have a beer," he said, without turning his head.

"Believe I'll try the Jack Daniel's," I said.

"Ain't as nourishin' as beer," he said. He turned as I put the gun away. "Why don't you show me how you work that thing? You as fast as old Wyatt?"

I left it in my pocket. "Not unless I intend to shoot someone." I went to the bar, poured bourbon into a glass. "Get you a beer, Swimmer?"

"I got part of one, but you might as well bring two, three more while you over there."

I took two Dortmunders out of the refrigerator and uncapped them, took them over and put them on the table in front of Swimmer, sat in the other leather chair and tasted my drink. He drained the bottle he had, picked up one of the fresh ones and drank half of it. "I thought I left the door locked," I said.

"Got me a key. I fish out here some. Kit's good enough to let me use it. Kit's a damn good man." He drank the other half of the beer, put the bottle on the floor beside his chair where he already had five empties. He had been there awhile. "Fred was a damn good man, too."

Could he have talked to Kit already? "How do you know about Fred, Swimmer?"

"Somebody told me."

"Wilson?"

"Kit must've gone out to the Pinnacle Club to find this

beer for you," he said. "I don't know of no other place around that has it. Now if I saw Tug and didn't make no citizen's arrest or at least call the law and say I had seen 'im, I would be a accessory. That's my long legal trainin' talkin'.'"

"Do you know what happened, Swimmer?"

He began on the second bottle. I didn't know beer could leave a bottle that fast. "We'll say it come over the smoke-signal circuit. Sure, Jud, I know, more'n you and Kit know."

"What?" I asked.

He put down that empty bottle. "You should've brung three," he said. "What happened was that Tug was sleepin' the sleep of the innocent in that there cell when somebody opened it up, which woke 'im up, then run before Tug could tell who done it, so Tug went out to ask Fred what the hell was goin' on and found Fred dead. Now maybe Tug should've stayed there, but I ain't gonna argue that because I know how good the hills look when a Indian is in trouble. Tug done what looked best to 'im; he run."

"How did he get to you?"

"Tug has got, at last count, forty-three cousins in Catherton. All forty-three of 'em has got cars."

"Do you believe him?" I asked.

"Enough to have another beer on it," he said. He got out of the chair and went to the kitchen, opened three beers and came back, carrying them in one hand.

I drank half my bourbon. "Do you know where he is?"

"Not now."

"Could you find him? Kit told the state men he would ask you for help."

"Might be I could, Jud. Ain't sure I will, even to help out Kit." His equanimity didn't amaze me, because, on my last trip, I had begun to know Swimmer; he would be rock calm in the middle of a major earthquake. That's not too good a metaphor; rocks are heaved all over in an earthquake, and Swimmer wouldn't be. "Tug ain't guilty."

"Kit doesn't think he is, either," I said. "Who is?" I wouldn't have been too surprised if he had given me an immediate, accurate answer.

"I don't know," he said. "I purely don't. I aim to find out."

"How, Swimmer?" I drank the last of my bourbon, went to the bar and poured another. The sky in the east had begun to grow its light-gray, predawn hue. I walked to the front window to watch for the first pastel blue.

"Well, we both know what Kit is doin' or tryin' his best to do—force somebody's hand all the way," he said.

"It's working," I said. "Do you know what happened yesterday afternoon?"

"About them two that come to visit you and left wishin' the hell they hadn't?"

"All right, you know."

He got up and came over to stand next to me, bringing his beer. "Cold beer and sunrise," he said. "Fine combination. Hope I see a lot more of both of 'em."

"How do you aim to find out?" I said.

"Same way Kit is tryin' to do it, only we are gonna accelerate things some. More'n some. You busy tonight?"

"This one or the one that's coming?"

"This one's over. The one that's comin'. Now, I wouldn't want you to miss any of the fun, so I thought we might go up to Lake City."

"Kit and I've been up there."

"I know that. You went up there polite as a Sunday afternoon tea."

"You don't intend to."

"Us blanket asses ain't learned how to crook our little fingers."

The minute of perfect pale blue ended, and light red-gold banded the deep-blue hills. A clear day after the rain had washed the way for it. "Are they open up there on Sunday nights?"

"Man we're goin' to see keeps a eight-day week," he said. He stretched mightily. It made an awesome sight.

"You weighed lately, Swimmer?"

"Have to go down to the cotton gin scales to do that and it's been closed since July."

"Last time I went out with you at night I had to run to the rescue."

"You bring that little old knife along when we blossom out amongst 'em tonight, too."

"Will we be that impolite?"

"It is possible. Us drunk Indians have got to have our sleep. You mind if I use one of the couches?"

"Do you snore?"

"Like a bull buffalo."

"Good. Me too."

TEN

The telephone awakened me, its ring cutting through a dream in which I tried again and again to play a tape recorder that had only one spool, and I filed the dream in my conscious mind because I had the feeling I would need it later. The sun was well up, and the lake glistened. My watch said ten. "Hello."

"Kit, Jud. You seen Swimmer?"

At the other end of the room from me Swimmer bulked under an Indian blanket like a small cruiser under a winter tarpaulin. "I see him now, on the far couch. How did you know he'd be here?" The sun hadn't yet warmed the room, and I shivered a little when I sat on one of the wooden bar stools in my shorts.

"He now and then holes up out there. He awake?"

"You awake, Swimmer?" I yelled.

"Ugh," Swimmer grunted.

"He's speaking Indian," I told Kit.

"Git 'im outta the sack."

113

"It's Kit, Swimmer," I said.

Swimmer sat up on the couch and the blanket fell to his waist; his hairless brown chest must have been three—make it three and a half—feet wide. "Tell 'im he'll have to call my secatary to make hisself a appointment." Swimmer talked at least three languages: courtroom, Cherokee and deep Oklahoman. This morning it was Oklahoman.

"Listen, Jud," Kit said. "I'm over at Billy Joe's office. I got Bessie down here this mornin'. She told me Fred borried that recorder yestiddy because he found some of Ben's tapes in a vault in the courthouse basement. I had forgot about that old vault, but Fred hadn't."

"Did she hear what was on the tapes?" I asked.

"No. Fred must've wanted to do 'er all by hisself, God rest his soul." Kit's benediction sounded natural.

"Who knew he found them?"

"Well, Bessie and the rest of the gals on the third floor knew it, so I guess about half the county found out about it," Kit said.

"Whoever shot him must have taken them," I said.

"It does look that way. Swimmer got hisself awake yet?"

"He wants you," I told Swimmer. He got up, stretched, scratched, and padded across to me. I gave him the phone. He said something into it in Cherokee, waited, then laughed. I walked around the service bar and began to make coffee.

"You knew he would, Kit," Swimmer said. "No. I didn't ask who drove 'im; didn't want to know. Sure he is, way deep back in there by now." He waited a minute. "Not today. Well, sure they pushin' you, but not today. Maybe later. Anyhow, he didn't do it. No, he didn't see who did. Like I told Jud, somebody woke 'im up openin' the cell door, then run. What? It's dark back there; you know that, and old Tug sleeps hard and wakes up hard, specially after he's had a long day gittin' beat on. Wait a minute."

He put down the phone, came around to the refrigerator, took out a beer, opened it, and drank contentedly, went back to the phone. "All right, Kit. I doubt if'n he'll come out. Would you if'n you was him? Me, neither. They'll damn sure believe you if'n they start into the hills after 'im. I'll maybe try 'er later on. Us Christian Indians don't work none on Sunday. I'll give you back to Jud." He finished the beer, handed me the phone, turned to get another one.

"Hello, Kit," I said. "I'm coming in after a while."

"No need," he said. "It's wilder'n a Baptist church squabble. They fixin' to organize manhunts, callin' in airplanes that will look at a lot of treetops, which won't do no good, because Tug ain't liable to climb no tree and wave at 'em. Might be better if you stay out there, Jud. Whyn't you and Swimmer go fishin'?"

"We might," I said. "You're not planning on going back up north tonight, are you?"

"Doubt if I git the time. I'll see you." He hung up.

Swimmer, drinking his second beer, turned on the television set. He tuned in a minister, intoning solemnly from some Tulsa pulpit. He listened while I poured my perked coffee, then began to rumble—in tune: "Bringin' in the sheaves, bringin' in the sheaves. We will come re-joicin' bringin' in the sheaves." He turned off the set, changed songs, "When the roll is called up yonder, when the roll . . ."

"You always drink beer for breakfast and sing hymns at the same time?" I asked.

"Only on Sundays." He went into the bathroom and sang while he splashed, came out and poured himself coffee. "You need a shave, white eyes," he told me. "That's one place we got it all over you."

"Don't you have to shave?" I remembered that I had read somewhere that most Indians don't.

"Us Indians have evoluted further'n you hairy-faced types."

He had dressed when I came back from my shave and shower. "Did Kit want you to try to find Wilson?" I asked him.

"Sounded like he did. Prob'ly somebody was listenin', and Kit had to sound that way."

"Are you going to?"

"Maybe later on, if'n it makes good sense to me later on," he said.

"It doesn't make sense now?"

"Not to this Indian."

"What if the state boys go after him and find him. They might have to kill him. From what I saw of him yesterday, and from what Mercer said last night, I would bet they kill him."

"What if they find him? What if I fly away from this here palace instead of drivin' away in my old truck, which I am now fixin' to do." He put down his cup and started for the door. "I thank you for your hospitality."

"Are we still going up to Lake City tonight?" I asked.

"You count on a interestin' evenin', friend. I will be back about two hours after the sun sets. Nine, ten o'clock." He flapped his massive hand at me, opened the door, and walked down the steps. I went out on the sun deck and watched him drive away.

I had a long day, but I got through it. About six I got hungry, had two drinks of the Jack Daniel's, which made me hungrier, climbed into my Corvette, and drove to town.

Ma was glad to see me. "Thought you'd gone and switched to a fancier eatin' place." she said.

"This is the fanciest and finest," I said.

"I saved two steaks for you and Kit. He oughtta be in." She started her skillet-heating process, then poured herself a cup of coffee to go with mine. She turned to me, her big face tight, her blue eyes clouded with concern. "I went to church this mornin'," she said, "and, while I was down on my knees, I did the prayin' I told you I'd do. I been doin' it ever' day, but I didn't pray for Fred—and this mornin' it was too late."

"Fred did the best he could in a hard business, Ma," I said. I should have been able to do better, but all epitaphs are inane in one way or another.

"Kit's doin' the best he can in the same business, and you right involved yourself," she said. "You think Caleb shot Fred and let Tug out?"

"It would make sense to think it."

She looked at me keenly. "If Kit thought so, he'd be back in the hills after them, no matter how tough they say it is in there. What about them tapes Fred found at the courthouse yestiddy?"

"Where'd you hear that?" I asked.

"Ever'body in town knew it a hour after he found 'em," she said. She served me a salad, put chopped potatoes on the grill to hash brown, slapped the steak in her skillet.

The kitchen back door that was framed between the refrigerator and the grill opened, and Kit came in. He swung up the hinged portion of the counter, came through, and took the stool next to mine. He looked tired. "Parked the car out back so's to git me some peace," he said. "Ever' damn body in town has either talked to me already or wants to."

"Where you been all day?" Ma asked him.

" 'Round and about. Thought you wasn't comin' in," he said to me.

"I got hungry."

"They tryin' for Tug?" Ma asked Kit.

"Not yet, not on foot. I wouldn't be here if they was.

Them airplanes didn't see nothin' but trees. Eight of 'em in here from Oklahoma City, not countin' Mercer and James."

"Men or airplanes?" I asked.

"Men. Two airplanes."

"What's next?" I asked.

"Find out tomorrow. Swimmer say anything to you about goin' in to talk to Tug?"

"Said he might later on," I said.

"Later on's liable to mean three weeks from now to a Indian, even Swimmer." He began to eat the salad Ma had set out for him. "Let's eat now." Talk didn't appeal to him this evening. When we had finished our dinners, he opened the counter section and held it up for me.

"My car's out front," I said.

"Leave it; we'll pick it up later."

"Thanks for the steak, Ma," I said.

"You welcome," she said. "Your tongue broke, old man?"

"I'm thinkin', Charity," Kit said. I followed him through the door into a shallow storeroom and out through another door into a narrow passageway between buildings. I looked up and saw that the sky had darkened. Kit's car was parked at the side of the alley, the passenger side nearest us. I got in while Kit walked around and climbed into the driver's seat, found his keys in his pocket, and inserted one into the ignition lock.

Concussion slapped the car and shook it, and a dull, thudding explosion magnified itself in the close interior. Dust and smoke exploded from the floor into a blinding swirl.

I found the door handle and was surprised when the door swung open easily. I threw my knees to the side and jumped clear of the car, turned, and saw Kit's head and shoulders across the car's top. He had jumped clear, too.

Smoke began to dissipate. The hood of the car had been pushed up. Other than that, it looked normal. It hadn't been much of an explosion; the windshield was still intact.

"You all right?" I yelled at Kit. My voice sounded thin after the blast.

"I'm some mad," he said, "but then I am also more than some thankful."

We met at the front of the car. The acrid, penetrating odor of exploded dynamite met us. I had an irrelevant, quick memory of the Fourth of July. "Either somebody didn't want to kill me, or some damn dummy tried to," Kit said. "Small charge down under the engine block in the front end. Sprung the hood up and wrecked the fan, not much else."

He looked under the hood closely, reached over and pulled loose something white from the top of the air filter, brought it out into the dusk, held it close to his eyes, and then passed it to me. A piece of Scotch tape was still attached to the white note: *See how easy it would be.*

"They right, too," Kit said. "Easy as fallin' off a log."

Ma came out of the passageway, hurried to Kit and put her hand on his shoulder, needing to feel what she saw. "Oh, Lord," she said. "I heard it and I knew. But you all right, both of you."

"Not much more'n a firecracker," Kit said. "Somebody playin' a joke."

"It didn't have to be," she said. "Might not have been."

"Was," Kit said. "Guess we'll take your car, Jud. Leave this'n here." He led the way back to the café, his steps quick and purposeful.

"Where you goin'?" Ma asked him.

"Just over to the office."

"Up north?"

"Not tonight," he said.

"You promise, Kit?"

119

"I said not tonight."

"Jud, you hold 'im to that," Ma said.

"I'll try," I said. I was still sorting thoughts; that came hard when the uppermost thought was that there could have been a heavy charge up behind the engine next to the fire wall and to Kit and me. I don't mind violence or danger when they have personality I can understand, identity I recognize. This had been a flaunting of impersonal, almost contemptuous power, leashed only as long as someone unseen wanted to keep it leashed. I felt delayed reaction in the pit of my stomach, felt it rise into my chest and change to full anger. If Kit had wanted to go up north, I would have been eager to go with him. I hadn't told Ma the truth.

Kit turned at the front door and looked at Ma, who leaned against the counter, her face still white. "Don't worry, Charity," he said.

"I'll worry," she said. "My God, how I'll worry."

We got into the Corvette and drove to Kit's office. Frank sat behind the desk in the outer room. No one else was there.

"Where'd ever'body go?" Kit asked.

"Back to the motel to git dinner," Frank said.

"They be in later?"

"Didn't say."

We went on into Kit's office. He sat down behind his desk, opened the drawer and pulled out a new, full bottle of moonshine. "We can both use one," he said. We both had one. He put away the bottle and picked up the phone, dialed.

"Clarice," he said. "Git me the Paradise Club up at the lake." He reached into the top right-hand drawer of the desk while he waited, took out a worn black belt and holster that held a long-barreled .38 on a heavy frame. "Time to git back in harness," he said to me. "I don't hold with carryin' one of these less'n it is gonna be needed. Now I can't shoot no dynamite, but I will damn sure shoot anybody gits in my way while I try to find out who's usin' dynamite." He listened a moment. "This is Marlow," he said. "Git Jack for me." He waited several seconds. "Jack, this is Kit. I told you the other night things was closed down. You figger I have changed or am gonna change my mind, maybe have it changed for me? No. I just had me a delayed Fourth of July celebration. You got a idea what I'm talkin' about? All right, maybe you don't. Pass the word: things are gonna stay closed down. I'll give you tonight and tomorrow, one day. Git the machines out and gone, the crap tables cleared out. I don't give a damn; you pass it around. Add this: I just strapped on my gun. That's all, Jack." He hung up the phone, leaned back in his chair and gazed at his ceiling. "I don't believe old Jack knew about it," he told me, "but then he is a damn good poker player."

"More pressure, then," I said. It was what I would have done.

"More. Federal pressure if'n I need to. Jack has got a U.S. gamblin' stamp; couple of 'em up there don't. One way or another, it will be gittin' 'ready to explode for keeps about this time tomorry."

"I don't like that word explode," I said.

"Me, neither," he said. "There will be nothin' more tonight. Whyn't you go on back out and git you some sleep?"

"You want me out of here."

"State boys'll be comin' back for a conference, Jud. They don't take kindly to you gentlemen of the press."

"All right, Kit. I am not helping."

"Helps to have somebody to talk to. And you ain't through yet."

ELEVEN

A full moon shone benignly as I drove to the cabin. I hurried because it was after nine and I didn't want to miss anything that Swimmer had in mind. He had said he intended to discard politeness; I had seen him do that once before in a few seconds of intense action. After the blast in Kit's car, I felt ready for that kind of action, with somebody else on the receiving end. Swimmer's pickup wasn't in sight when I parked behind the house and sat in my car for a minute or two, listening to the night sounds.

I got out, went up the steps and into the cabin, turned on the lights and made myself a drink. I listened carefully for car wheels; after yesterday afternoon, no more cars would pull in without my being ready for them. When I heard one, after about thirty minutes, I went out on the sun deck, out of the light that came through the windows and the door. It was Swimmer. He got out of his pickup, came up, and said, "I see you over there in the dark, only it ain't dark because that is a real Indian summer moon."

"See-oh, ta-heej," I said. It means hello, friend; I had learned it in June. That and "choots," which is boy, and "gahooch," which is girl, and "shooo," which can mean anything and everything, were the extent of my Cherokee.

"See-oh," he said. "Any beer left?"

"I doubt it," I said. "You spent the morning here."

"Let's go in and find out," he said. He took two bottles from the refrigerator and opened them, leaned on the service bar. I sat on one of the stools. "You go in town to eat?" he asked.

I told him I had and described the blast in Kit's car, repeated Kit's conversation with Simmons.

He drank half a beer. "Then they was warnin' Kit," he said. "They might as well warn a wall."

"A moving wall," I said. "Kit strapped on his gun."

"Maybe time he did," Swimmer said. "Well, that makes this trip we gonna take after bit a little more worthwhile. You ever had to bend the law a little, white eyes?"

"I've bent it some," I said.

"Figgered you had." He started on his second beer.

"Are we going to tonight?"

"Might need to," he said. He finished his beer. "You about ready?"

"I'm ready." I had nursed along the anger I had felt after the explosion, after I had read the warning note.

"Come on then."

I turned out the lights and locked the door as we left. "Do you want to take my car?" I asked.

"Doubt I could git all of me in there," he said. I doubted it, too. "We'll take my old truck. It ain't far."

Swimmer drove the pickup at sixty when we got on the highway, and we got to Lake City a little after eleven, went through the town and north a half mile, parked in front of a neon sign that said INDIAN INN.

"You sure you ready?" Swimmer asked.

"Maybe I ought to know for what," I said.

He grinned hugely at me. The red from the neon reached into the front seat and turned his brown face to bronze. "We gonna influence some people who are liable to take a good deal of influencin'," he said. "I figger you will be able to keep up. Just do what comes natural."

The inside of the place was about the same as that of the Paradise Club, a little smaller, a little less welcoming. A coin-operated pool table stood at one end of the big room, light flooding onto it from an overhead cone. Two men and two women were playing, laughing. The crowd wasn't large, about twelve people along with the pool players. They all looked as if they had come in from a day of boating, and they probably had. Swimmer and I sat at the bar. "Hey, Elvin," he said to the man who came to us, "give us two beers, two apiece." Elvin, short and squat, light-haired and ugly, brought them. The jukebox played a Glen Campbell record. "That old Arkansaw boy can fairly well pick and sing, can't he, Elvin?" Swimmer said.

"Hell, they all sound the same after awhile," Elvin said.

"You got a tin ear," Swimmer said. "I don't see Hirsh. He around?"

"Up to his house," Elvin said.

"Whyn't you call 'im and tell 'im to come on down?" Swimmer said.

"Hirsh don't like bein' called."

"Bein' as it's me that wants 'im, he won't mind none," Swimmer said.

"Hell, he don't even like you, Swimmer," Elvin said. He might win prizes for honesty, not for tact. "You know that as well as I do."

"Well, now, that might be why I'm here. Prob'ly is. Want to smoke the peace pipe."

"That'll be the damn day," Elvin said.

"Suppose you go ahead on and give it a try," Swimmer said. He drained one of his beers, not bothering with the glass Elvin had set out, picked up the other bottle.

The bartender looked at Swimmer awhile, trying to figure this out and obviously not being able to, went down the back bar and used the telephone at its end. He came back. "He said he'll be down after while," he said. He went to the other end of the bar.

"Me and Hirsh have had us a couple difficulties about civil rights," Swimmer said to me. "Me and Elvin, too, for that matter."

"I don't see any of your Indian buddies in here," I said. The last time I had gone out with Swimmer he had taken me to an Indian bar where he held court for petitioners.

"Hirsh don't like Indians," he said. "They ain't got enough money to spend in that back room that is behind that door you can see down there past Elvin."

"Gambling?"

"It looks like gamblin'. It ain't. It is a sure way for old Hirsh to git hisself rich."

"Crooked?" I asked.

"As a rickety dog's hind leg. I once made old Hirsh cough up three relief checks he taken off'n a old buddy of mine who couldn't say seven in English if he'd ever of seen one at Hirsh's table, which he damn sure didn't."

The jukebox quit, and Swimmer got up from his bar stool, walked over to it and put in two quarters, punched buttons, and came back. Another Campbell record, "Burning Bridges Behind Me," began. "I do like country music," Swimmer said.

"That's not country," I said.

"Is the way he sings it." He turned his head toward the back of the room, and I looked in that direction with him. Three men came through the back door, stopped in a cluster, and looked around the room and at us. Two of them sat down in one of the rear booths. The third stopped to talk to the bartender briefly and then came on down behind the bar to us.

He looked forty, a hard forty, and he was about as big as I, probably ten pounds heavier because he had begun to turn to fat, not sloppily, not yet; I could still see his muscle. Hard, green eyes straddled a hooked nose that gave the upper part of his face a dominating look, but his mouth didn't conform; it was small, the lips surprisingly red and mobile. I don't like men with small mouths.

"You want to see me?" he said to Swimmer. "I got nothin' to talk to you about. You got nothin' to git on me about."

"Have a beer with me and my friend here, Hirsh," Swimmer said. "I am buyin'."

"I don't drink beer."

"Owner of a fine, plush place like this'n prob'ly wouldn't," Swimmer said. "Would prob'ly have scotch. Whyn't you pour you one of them?"

"How come, Swimmer? I ain't got time to waste on you." He watched Swimmer warily, studied me with quick side glances.

"Sure you have, but I ain't gonna impose on your time too much. You hear about old Tug?"

"I heard about the bastard. Ever'body has heard about 'im."

"You figger he done it?"

"Sure he done it."

"You hear about old Annie down to Catherton?" Swimmer asked, his voice a little harder.

"I heard," Hirsh said. "That damn Marlow has got no call."

"You hear about a boy with a broke arm and another'n with a injury to his knife arm?" Swimmer's voice was still low but his words had bite to them.

"Maybe I did," Hirsh said. He looked at me directly, carefully for the first time. "This'n the one?"

Swimmer answered his question with a question, a lawyer's device. "You hear the sheriff is gonna need a new front end for his car?"

"I don't know what the hell you're talkin' about or leadin' up to," Hirsh said. "And I am gittin' tired of listenin'."

Swimmer leaned forward, his elbows on the bar. "You send them two with Annie to see my friend here?" he asked.

Hirsh put his elbows against the back bar, looked down it at the bartender and at the two he had left in the back booth. His mouth moved, pursed, and uneasiness became apparent in his eyes. "Annie done all that herself," he said.

"Annie don't carry that much weight," Swimmer said. "If there is a pipeline from here to Joplin and Kansas City, you the end of it. Comes out here and goes in here. Jack and the rest of 'em pay the dues, but Jack don't head things up anymore. You the one swingin' the muscle."

"I told you I don't know what the hell you talkin' about," Hirsh said.

"Could you find out for me? Maybe from them two back there in the booth?"

Hirsh fidgeted visibly now. I took a drink of my beer, and my throat welcomed its coldness. "I had enough of your crap," Hirsh said.

"Me, too," Swimmer said. He punched out his next words the way a prosecuting attorney throws his climax question in cross examination. "I want to know who killed Fred. I want to know who killed Ben and Beth. I am fixin' to persuade you to tell me all you know about it."

"You crazy, blanket-ass son of a bitch," Hirsh said. He slid his right hand into the side pocket of his jacket, and, as he did, Swimmer leaned far over the bar, clamped one

127

hand on each of Hirsh's arms and heaved forward and upward. Hirsh came over the bar as if he had been propelled by jets. The black-leather sap he had gotten clear of his pocket but no farther fell from his hand to the top of the bar. Swimmer swung him to the floor, closed his right hand into a mallet and slammed Hirsh under the heart.

Hirsh made a choking noise in the back of his throat; I heard it clearly over the noise from the jukebox. His eyes rolled up and back, and Swimmer dropped him to the floor in time to meet the concerted rush of the two from the back booth. "You git Elvin," Swimmer yelled at me as he drove forward into the charge.

I had been expecting the violence; my reflexes had readied themselves with the expectation. Without thinking, I went up and over the bar. Elvin had wrenched open one of the cabinet doors in the back bar, and I saw his right hand close on a gun stock, saw the twin sawed shotgun barrels in front of it start to swing into the open. I reached him and clubbed him in the back of the neck with my right fist, felt the shock all the way up to my shoulder. He slammed face first into the cabinet door and slid on down to the duckboard walk behind the bar, didn't move. My hand ached from the blow. I should have used a beer bottle.

I heard a woman scream, short and high, and a man yell, "Out. Let's get out." I swung around and saw the crowd stampede for the front door, jam themselves up in it.

I saw that Swimmer had knocked both of the men down with his charge and had gone to his knees on the floor with the strength of his momentum. He and one of the men, the larger of the two, got to their feet at the same time. The man tucked his chin in behind his left shoulder, took a shuffling step in toward Swimmer and threw two good, straight punches, a short left and a long right. He hit

Swimmer squarely with his left, and Swimmer took it un-flinchingly, probably unknowingly, caught the right hand in his left the way an infielder instinctively catches a line drive at his eyes.

I saw his shoulder hunch with exerted power, and the man whose hand he held screamed, far louder than the woman had seconds before, and crumpled to his knees, clawing at Swimmer's rigid forearm and wrist with his free hand.

I came around the end of the bar in time to see the one left on the floor sit up, shake his head and start to go inside his coat to his armpit with his right hand. He was groggy, and I reached much faster than he, pressed the spring in my pants pocket and threw my gun into the open. I saw that I had time, so I didn't shoot. I took a step and slapped my gun barrel across the side of his head, hard. He folded back to the floor. I took his gun and remembered Elvin and the shotgun and went back to him. He hadn't moved. I pulled the shotgun clear of the cabinet and laid its barrels across the bar as the last of the crowd emptied through the front door.

Swimmer dropped the hand he had crushed, took a pistol from under the moaning man's coat and brought it to the bar with him.

Glen Campbell was still singing, something about Little Rock.

"Shooo," Swimmer said. His black eyes glittered and he grinned happily at me, looked over at Elvin and at the man I had hit with my gun. "You will damn sure do." One of his beers still stood on the bar. I had knocked mine over when I went after Elvin. He picked up the bottle and took a long drink, set it down and took the shotgun, broke it and dropped the shells to the floor. He closed the gun, took the stock in both hands and, like a hammer thrower, heaved it into the jukebox. The heavy barrels shattered bubbling plastic and brittle glass and records, and the singing stopped. He took the pistol he had brought with him to the bar and threw it into the mirror over the back bar. Heavy glass shards cascaded.

Swimmer picked up Hirsh from the floor in front of the bar, slapped his chest and waist and didn't find a gun. He dragged Hirsh by the back of his coat to the booth nearest the front door and propped him into its corner, then came back behind the bar with me. "You ever stack a place?" he said.

"No." I wasn't sure what he meant.

"Time you learned. I will need a little help. Take the other end." He squatted and put the palms of his hands flat against the protruding inner edge of the bar, and I saw what he intended to do, followed his cue. We strained together, and the back of the bar, his end first, tilted up, hung in the air, moved finally past the point of balance. The whole bar, twenty feet of it—and, from the feel, more than a ton of it—crashed out and down, a hell of a noise. Dust swirled heavily into the air.

I leaned against the back bar, the adrenalin almost gone from me through my effort. Swimmer didn't even breathe hard. "You ain't tired, are you? We got work to do."

He started at the back booths, on the tables that divided the facing seats, and he used the same technique he had used on the bar. He bent his knees, turned his palms upward, tensed, then heaved. The single, metal table legs came up from the floor with the excruciating squeal of bent and stripped screws and Swimmer tossed the table-tops into a loose pile in the center of the room. I went around to help him. We muscled the pool table onto its side, then over onto its top. Plastic balls rattled and rolled on the tile floor. We whipsawed the ends of the booth seats and pulled them away from the wall, added them to the growing pile of wreckage in the center of the room. We finished at the booth that held Hirsh, who was conscious, slumped forward with his head in his arms. "Now," Swimmer said to him. "What about all that crap you said you had had enough of?"

Hirsh rolled his head, finally raised it. "I don't know," he said thickly. He talked in a short gasp. Swimmer had broken his ribs.

"I will finish up, Jud," Swimmer said to me. "Whyn't you have you a beer." He walked to the door at the end of the bar, broke its lock with a kick, and turned on lights with a switch inside the room. I went over to watch.

The setup wasn't up to Las Vegas standards, but it made a good miniature try. I saw a dice table, a semicircular blackjack table with a slot for the dealer, a wheel, six slot machines along one section of the wall.

Swimmer kicked in the felt-covered bottom of the dice table, then turned it over and wrenched off one of its thick legs. He used the leg to wreck the slot machines, swinging it the way Mantle swung a bat. Quarters spilled and streamed to the floor. He used the leg on the wheel; it would never spin again. He walked into the dealer's slot at the blackjack table and tore it loose from the floor, slammed it over against the dice table. He looked around with satisfaction. "That about does it," he said. He came back to the outer room and went to Hirsh.

"Who?" Swimmer asked.

"Honest to Christ, I don't know," Hirsh said thickly.

"Don't know what?"

"Don't know about Alexander and the girl and Peters."

"But you sent them two along with Annie, didn't you?"

"I sent 'em," Hirsh said.

"Where'd you git 'em?"

"They come down here from Coffeyville."

"They syndicate?" Swimmer asked, as calm as he would have been in a courtroom. He still hadn't worked up a sweat.

"Claimed to be," Hirsh said.

"How about the dynamite in Kit's car?" Swimmer asked.

"Don't know." He tried to sit up and the pain of his movement pushed him back into his bent, old-man's posture.

"I would hate to pound any on a hurt man," Swimmer said, "but I am ready to start."

"I had it done," Hirsh said.

"Anybody tell you to?"

"No."

"Where did them two you had with you tonight come from?" Swimmer said.

"Joplin."

"They syndicate?"

"No," Hirsh said. "Just a couple said they was guns."

"They maybe was," Swimmer said. "Now they ain't."

Precaution is a friend to a winner. I went away from Swimmer and Hirsh and to the bar to check on Elvin. He was sitting up. I helped him to his feet and around to the booth that held Hirsh, the only one still intact. He slumped into the opposite seat. "I'd rather have him where I can see him," I said. The one I had hit with my gun was still out. The one Swimmer had handled lay on the floor, apparently passed out. A broken hand hurts worse than a broken leg.

"You been pretending to be syndicate, ain't you?" Swimmer said to Hirsh.

"I got connections," Hirsh said.

"You got shit," Swimmer said. "You got 'em fooled, even Jack, but you only makin' a try at bein' big time." The profanity sounded incongruous, even after I had seen a measure of his capacity for violence. "I will tell you once. You fool with any more of my friends, any way, I will come after you, and I will make tonight look like a ice-cream social. You hear me?"

"I hear you," Hirsh said.

"Come on, Jud," Swimmer said. I followed him through the front door, stopped and looked back at the place. I found it hard to believe, but I had to believe it.

"Are you going to leave him a front door?" I asked Swimmer.

"Guess I might as well not," Swimmer said. He reached and took hold of the outer top corner of the door with both hands, swung his weight and his strength down and out. The door hinges tore out of the jamb. He let it fall to the gravel of the front yard, turned and walked to his pickup. I followed. We got in. Two cars were still parked in the lot, and a little knot of people standing between them watched us drive away.

Swimmer didn't talk for the first couple of miles, but he laughed twice to himself and once reached over and punched me gently in the shoulder. "You and Kit thought you was takin' on the organization, didn't you now?"

"Yes. It still looks that way to me," I said.

"Looks more to me like it was old Hirsh pretendin' he was one of 'em."

"He could have been lying, Swimmer," I said. "I would hate to lie to you, but, if I were Hirsh, I would do it before I would involve the syndicate if I knew they didn't want to be involved." I respected Swimmer and was willing to give him full credit for finding out who had sent the two to me and who had planted the dynamite in Kit's car, but I had to doubt that he knew enough about the ways of the Mafia, about the surety of their punishments for sins against them.

133

"Maybe you right," he said. He thought about it for several miles. "We will prob'ly find out, and now there'll be three of us—me as well as you and Kit."

"You are welcome to the group," I said. "There going to be any trouble with Kit about what we did tonight?"

"Why would there be trouble?"

"We tore up a lot of private property."

"Hell, we had to, defendin' ourselves. You don't think Hirsh would have guts enough to go to the law, to Kit, do you?"

"No. I guess he wouldn't."

"He damn sure wouldn't. Besides, stackin' bars is one of the onliest recreations us backwoods types is allowed."

"I'm glad the custom hasn't spread," I said.

"When do you aim to do that story on us underprivileged Cherokees?" he said.

"Any time you want it done."

"I will start preparin' you a brief," he said. "I hope there's plenty beer left in your icebox. Stackin' a place always leaves me thirstier'n hell."

When we got there, I opened three Dortmunders for him, poured a very healthy Jack Daniel's for myself.

TWELVE

Swimmer had dressed and made coffee when I awakened Monday morning, and he brought me a cup when I swung my feet to the floor. It was only seven-thirty.

"Things to do; places to go," he said.

"Thought you decided we did it all last night," I said.

"I thought some more."

I drank some of the coffee; it came on as strong as Swimmer had the night before. "Like what?" I said.

"Fred's funeral's at eleven," Swimmer said.

"I'll want to go."

"I want to," he said. "Can't. Old Fred would understand."

"How come you can't, Swimmer?" I had begun to talk Oklahoman.

"All the law'll be there. That's the time for me to be up north."

"With Wilson?"

"With some kinfolk of Tug's." He drained his coffee

cup—no beer this morning—rinsed it with hot water from the faucet and set it upside down on the steel drainboard.

Intuition asked for me: "The boy? What did Kit call him? Caleb."

Swimmer looked at me admiringly. "You a shaman," he said. "You have heard the turtle."

"What?"

"The turtle talks to selected Cherokees," he said, "so they hear things others don't."

"What about Caleb?" I got off the daybed and followed him as he walked to the door.

"I hear the turtle, too. I will see you." He went through the door and down the steps, and I noticed that it's true: Indians do walk slightly pigeon-toed; at least Swimmer did.

I shaved, showered and dressed, with a tie, the first I had worn since I had gotten to Oklahoma. I drove by Ma Maxwell's; the café was closed. Frank, at the undersheriff's desk, said Kit had gone home to dress for Fred's funeral, would probably be back to the office before he went to the church. He introduced me to a short, husky, gray-haired man in a sports coat, Sam Ballard, Catherton's bondsman; Kit had mentioned him.

"Is anyone up at Fred's house?" I asked Frank.

"Son that come in from Texas yestiddy afternoon is stayin' up there," Frank said. "You and Kit had you a close one last night, didn't you?"

"Depends on the way you look at it," I said. "I will be back in twenty or thirty minutes."

"You goin' up to Fred's?"

"Might do that," I said.

"How come?"

"I thought of something," I said. I left, drove out to a café I had seen on the highway and drank coffee for a quarter of an hour, then went back to the City-County building.

Kit had called, Frank said, and had told him to tell me, if I came in, that he would see me at the church. Ballard was still there.

"I can't make the funeral," I told Frank. "Is that tape recorder that Fred had the other night here?"

"No," he said. "They dusted it for prints and all they found was Fred's, so Kit took it on back over to Ben's— Billy Joe's—office. Why?"

"I want to borrow it," I said. "I'll go on over there. Tell Kit I'm sorry I missed the funeral, but I've got something I have to do."

"I'll tell 'im," Frank said.

I walked to the courthouse and rode the slow elevator to the third floor. Briggs's secretary was at her desk, and two other women sat on a chrome and vinyl sofa, talking to her. "Billy Joe's already left for the funeral, Mr. Blade," she said.

"I need a favor," I said.

"Sure," she said. "Mr. Blade's from *Now* magazine," she told the two.

"I'd like to borrow a tape recorder, the one that Fred had borrowed."

"Why, I guess that'd be all right," she said. "Billy Joe doesn't use it." She got up from her chair and took the recorder out of a credenza that stood against the wall.

"Thank you, Bessie," I said.

"You're welcome, Mr. Blade. Will you want to keep it very long?"

"No. I'll take it out to Kit's cabin and have it back this evening or tomorrow morning."

"There's only the one spool on it. Do you have a tape?" she asked. She wanted desperately to ask why I wanted the recorder, but her innate southwestern courtesy kept her curiosity in partial check.

"I found . . . I have a tape," I said. "Thank you again."

As I closed the door behind me, I saw the three of them begin to talk excitedly.

Bessie and the two women with her and Frank and the bondsman made five I had baited. Frank might not talk a lot, but I've yet to see a bondsman who didn't make much of his way with early inside information and I already knew how efficiently and quickly Bessie and her third-floor friends could spread word; it wasn't yet eleven, but by one or two half the county would know where I had been that morning, what I had done and what I was, ostensibly, going to do.

I stopped at a supermarket east of Catherton and bought two cases of beer—they didn't have Dortmunder—and a loaf of bread, then drove on to the cabin, slowly, because I wanted to savor this part of the day and its sunny peace. I heard my turtle, and Swimmer heard his. That's a peculiar piece of Indian heritage. Would it be mythology; did Indians have a mythology? Religion? *Song of Solomon:* ". . . and the voice of the turtle is heard in our land." I would have to ask Swimmer more about it. I wondered which of our turtles sang truly. I didn't have any dire premonitions, but I did have a sure feeling that trip twenty-one had about come to its end. I hoped I hadn't overestimated my ability to be around at its end. I have a fault: I'm patient only to a point.

I unloaded the beer and put it in the refrigerator; Swimmer had left four Dortmunders, and I had one of those with my noon sandwich. I got the news on television. The newscaster said a manhunt for Wilson was continuing, dogs were being brought to Catherton from the state prison that afternoon, and Crime Bureau officials expected to have further news momentarily. He said Sheriff Kit Marlow had no comment.

I probably should have gone to Fred's funeral; I would

have had time, but no other ceremony is more useless or more barbaric. Weddings run a distant second.

Kit called at one. "You tryin' to be a damn fool or a hero?" he asked.

"Neither," I said. "Listen, a man named Hirsh from Lake City put . . ."

"I know," he said. "Swimmer come by about eight. Then you come by later. Then you went up to Fred's, except you didn't go up to Fred's, and then you made damn sure ever'body in the county would find out you borried a tape recorder. I can't git out there 'till evenin', if then, Jud."

"No need for you to."

"Maybe not. I will hope not. Borryin' the recorder is just another raise in the table stakes, ain't it?"

"That's all."

"Swimmer says it ain't syndicate."

"He hears his turtle; I hear mine," I said.

"You been in the Daniel's?" he said.

"Not yet."

"Jud, whyn't you come on back into town for the rest of the day. I would appreciate it if you would do that little thing for me."

"I'd waste all my morning's work. Did Swimmer say anything to you about Caleb Wilson?"

"Not this mornin'. But last night, before him and you decided to play stack with Hirsh, he was up north to Pete's Corner, and he was huntin' Caleb, not Tug."

"Does that mean anything to you?" I asked.

"Hell, yes, it does. Caleb is a mean young bastard, a lot meaner'n Tug's ever been. I had 'is name high on my list 'fore you and me got on this other track."

"Would he have shot Fred?"

"I still think he would've hit Fred in the head or

locked 'im up in Tug's place, but I ain't a authority on Caleb. Swimmer is, or will be 'fore the day's over. They yellin' at me from out front, Jud. I gotta go."

"After Wilson?"

"After all these damn fools and dogs that are goin' after 'im. I will be out there when I can git out there."

"I'll be here when you come."

"You got your little old gun?" he asked.

"I've got it."

"Stay real loose and careful, Jud," he said. He hung up.

I opened another beer and went out onto the sun deck, decided to go down to the fishing dock. I sat on the planked walkway and listened to tiny waves lap against the tin of the boat house, watched small perch strike at my cigarette butt when I threw it into the quiet backwater. I wondered if Kit would sell me this place, or half of it. I decided I would ask him. I went back up the path.

Two men, well dressed in gray, stood at the foot of the steps, facing me. Neither wore a hat. One looked about fifty, possibly fifty-five; his hair gleamed iron gray and he looked as if he had just come from a barber shop; his skin was white, with a look of transparency, his eyes dark. His features were regular, in no way remarkable, but he had a look of remoteness and dedication that would have caused him to stand out in any crowd, even though he was small, not more than five seven.

The second man was young, thirty, larger than the other, but inches shorter than I, fifty pounds lighter. He had sandy hair, blue-gray eyes, an even tan.

I had put my hand casually into my pocket. I kept it there. Both seemed unusually careful to keep their hands in my sight.

"Mr. Blade?" the younger one asked.

"Yes," I said.

"We would like to talk to you." He emphasized the "talk."

"All right."

"I'm Mr. Green. This is Mr. Brown." Mr. Brown nodded politely. "Could we go inside? Mr. Brown doesn't like the sun."

"I was about to ask you," I said. "Up those steps."

"Of course." Mr. Brown led the way and Mr. Green followed. They waited for me to open the door.

I took my hand out of my pocket and reached for the handle, and Mr. Green slid the sap from his sleeve and rapped me over my right ear. I saw the flicker of skillful movement, then spun down through soft grayness, not far from the edge of unconsciousness but never perilously near. Mr. Green caught me easily as I slumped. I could hear and feel but I couldn't see.

Mr. Brown opened the door and Mr. Green helped me to one of the big chairs. While I began to come slowly up into the real, stable world, he took my gun from my pocket, my knife from its sheath. I cupped my hand over the throb above my ear. Mr. Brown sat on the coffee table in front of me, and Mr. Green stood behind me.

"I apologize," Mr. Brown said. "I know you are proficient with the tools you carry, but I do not know how excitable or how impulsive you are. You won't be touched again."

The throb grew lighter, almost disappeared. "I'll appreciate that," I said.

"For conference purposes," he said, "I'll say that I represent certain business interests that have been exploring investments in this area and that you represent Mr. Marlow, or at least have ready access to him, which I do not." He didn't have an accent but his intonation was so precise that I was sure he must have overcome one.

"That's fair," I said. "Could I offer you gentlemen a drink?"

"No thank you, but Mr. Green will get you one if you like."

"In the bar," I said. "Don't bother about ice." Mr. Green went to the bar and brought me back three fingers of bourbon. I took half of it. The throb had left me now. "Does your company have a name?" I asked Mr. Brown.

"Several," he said. He didn't smile, but his word had humor in it. "And we have a large number of offices."

"Any near here?" I asked. I drank the rest of the bourbon. I could be as ambiguous as he. We both knew what we were talking about. I had known since the younger one had told me their names, the ones for the day.

"None," Mr. Brown said. "And we have decided not to establish any. That is part of the message I have for Mr. Marlow."

"Not even a branch?" I said.

"No. We have had some equipment here on an experimental lease basis. We have decided to terminate the lease, to recall the equipment."

"How about your salesmen?"

"We let a free-lance man or two come in on commission only. We have terminated them. You, Mr. Blade, played a part in the termination."

"What about contracts in this area?" I asked. "Did you ever let one?" Contract means one thing to a syndicate man.

"Mr. Alexander?"

"Yes," I said.

"No. None at all. You have my word."

I believed him. "Then you're not interested in another tape?"

"A what?"

"A tape for a recorder."

"No. I hadn't heard about it."

I, for no real reason, felt glad that there was something he didn't know, hadn't heard about. I guess I did have a reason: I'd hate to think people like this were omniscient. "Is there anything else, Mr. Brown?"

"You can, if you will, tell Mr. Marlow it will not be necessary to call for outside help. I'm a reactionary; I feel there is already too much federal influence." This time the humor was unmistakable.

"I'm sure you do," I said.

"And, I promise you, it would be a waste of time." He got up from his chair. "That's all, Mr. Blade. We'll be going."

"I'll leave your things in the seat of your car," Mr. Green said from behind me. "You can come out after them when we leave."

"Thank you," I said. What else would I have said? I wanted my knife and my gun back. Mr. Brown went down the steps, Mr. Green after him. I was tempted to hit Mr. Green in the back of his tanned and healthy neck, right above the middle of his immaculate white collar, highly but not foolishly tempted. I went down the steps when I had been told to, in time to see that they left in a black Chrysler, one of the large ones. Mr. Green had been truthful. I retrieved my knife and gun from the left front seat of my Corvette, feeling embarrassed that they had been taken from me so easily, thankful that I had them back.

I wondered if they had driven all the way from Kansas City; decided I would probably never know. I took some consolation from the fact that they, the ones who pushed buttons that sent impulses to the many tentacles, had sent the first string to me. Have no doubt about it; the two were first string.

I also felt relieved. Swimmer had been right last night.

Hirsh had been pretending he had syndicate power behind him, to strengthen his position in the local association, to take over from Simmons. The syndicate had sent its probe into the county through Hirsh, but had now decided to abandon him and the probe, at least for awhile. For Kit's sake, I hoped it would be forever, but that is a very long word. Now it wasn't Kit and Swimmer and I against the organization. The syndicate doesn't awe me, but I am a pragmatist; the FBI hasn't been enough to break it, not in all its years of trying, and Kit, Swimmer and I fall a little short of the FBI, at least in total resources.

I spent the rest of the afternoon wondering where the syndicate's disavowal and withdrawal had left us—me— and telling myself I had let Kit's faith in his knowledge of his people cloud the probable facts, that Wilson or his son, Caleb, had killed Alexander and his fiancée, and that Caleb had probably killed Fred. Swimmer knew them better than Kit and he had left that morning to find Caleb. He had said he had heard his turtle.

Kit drove in about five, parked and came up the steps and into the cabin. I told him about the afternoon, Mr. Brown and Mr. Green, and I'll admit, under duress, that I omitted the sapping and my disarmament.

"Repeat it for me, what he said," Kit said.

I did, and I could remember exact quotes from Mr. Brown. He had been convincing.

"You believe 'em?" he asked.

"I don't think they had any reason to lie," I said.

"They need a reason?" I felt the strength of his stubbornness. He had thought, had become convinced his pushing would force a silent power into the open, where he was equally convinced he could handle it. He still stood behind his judgment of Wilson.

"Maybe not, Kit. Best I can say is that I believed them."

"All right. I still don't think it was Tug. Caleb maybe. Swimmer ain't sure about Caleb." He went to the bar, got a glass and ice from the refrigerator and made himself a dark-brown bourbon and water, drank half of it. "Shooo, that store-bought booze is welcome."

"I don't understand Swimmer's outlook on Caleb," I said. "He told me the other night that Wilson had forty-three cousins in Catherton, all of them with cars. He intimated one of them drove Wilson, not Caleb."

"Did he say it was one of 'em?"

I thought back. Swimmer hadn't. "No, Kit, he didn't."

"You got to git used to Swimmer," Kit said. "He won't lie to you, but he'll step around the truth like a Mexican doin' a hat dance." He drank the rest of his bourbon and water. "Shooo, I had me a hard afternoon."

"Hunting Wilson?"

"I didn't git a chance to do no huntin'. First them state men, six of 'em, and a couple boys from McAlester took the dogs up to Tug's place, let 'em smell around and turned 'em loose. From then on she turned into—you ever see one of them Keystone Cop movies?"

"Sure."

"Compared to this afternoon, them cops was relaxed. Dogs run around the barn and the smokehouse three, four times, treed 'em a couple sows in the pig lot, run a mile or so to the pasture where Tug feeds his cattle, run back. Dogs wasn't winded, but the laws damn sure was. Then ever'body dragged up, down and around two, three mountains, and across six cricks 'till they got stopped by the river. They come back to the house and the cars, a hell of a lot slower than they went out. Two was missin'— men, not dogs. We blowed car horns until one of 'em come in. They was still blowin' and yellin' for the other'n when I left."

"Make me one of those while you're over there," I said

He did. "Do they have any hope of catching Wilson, Kit?"

"No. I mean they got hope but they ain't got chance."

"Can Swimmer find them?"

"He can find 'em—Tug and Caleb—and he can talk to 'em, but I doubt even Swimmer can bring 'em in."

"Can you?"

"Sure. My way, in my time. They all go on back to where they come from; let the hills git good and quiet, and, 'fore too long, Old Tug, or prob'ly Caleb first, will come out far enough to drink a little beer and talk a little, and I'll git 'em." He put another ice cube in his drink. "But that's the onliest damn way."

"We aren't getting much of anywhere," I said.

"Don't look like it. You said them two this afternoon didn't know anything about tapes for the recorder?"

"They said they didn't."

"Maybe you went through all that play actin' this mornin' for nothin'."

"Maybe I did at that," I said.

Kit walked out onto the sun deck, and I followed him. The sun had fallen low enough to begin shadow on our side of the lake, to gild the water on the far side. "You been down to look at my boat house yet?" he asked.

"I've been down," I said. "I've been tempted to take the boat out but I figured I don't know enough about one."

"Let's go on down and I'll show you," he said. We finished our drinks, put down our glasses, walked down the steep path and across the planked walk between shore and boathouse. Kit explained the engine to me, and I told him I might try a run in the morning. He took an ultralight rod and reel from the rack on the wall, one with a small, treble-hooked lure attached. "I'll heave this around the cove a time or two, see if'n I can raise me a buck bass." We went out on the catwalk that surrounded the boathouse on three sides.

We both heard the car pull in and stop at the cabin. Kit reeled in from a cast and leaned the rod against the boat-house wall. "Prob'ly Swimmer," he said. "He said he'd be out."

Someone yelled, "Blade!" He had apparently tried the door and had found no one there.

"I'll be damned," Kit said. "What's he doin' out here? I left 'im out to Tug's place. Down here!"

Haley Mercer came to the top of the path and looked down at us. "Come on up," he said.

Kit put his hand on my arm when I started to take a step. "Whyn't you come on down?" he said.

Mercer came, in a hurry, sliding on the gravel. He stepped on the plank walk, and I could see his anger. "Damn you, Blade, where's that tape?" he rasped.

THIRTEEN

"Thought you was out in the hills, Mercer," Kit said, "blowin' car horns for lost folks and trippin' over bloodhounds. How come you ain't?"

"I want that tape, Blade," Mercer said. He took a couple of steps toward me. "I'll decide later whether or not to charge you with suppressing evidence."

"What tape?" I said.

"Don't give me that shit. You know what tape." His eyes had always jumped around before. Now they bored at and into me. "I know you goddamn press people. Smart asses. Let you travel an inch and you try to run a mile. Marlow has let you run, Blade, but I told you once before I won't."

"Jud asked you what tape you talkin' about," Kit said.

"Has he given it to you, Marlow? You together in this? You've tried to screw me up all along." His anger burst visibly onto his face, and he didn't try to control it.

Anger or the frustrating rage of desperation? The two can and do become synonomous. "You're liable to be a goddamn has-been sheriff before you find out what hit you. I came out here to get that tape and I will. I want it now. Have you played it? Do you know what's on it?"

If Mercer was the fish we had baited, he would have to strike suddenly and hard. I moved toward him along the catwalk, farther away from Kit, separating the two of us as targets and trying to divide Mercer's attention. I didn't want him to strike yet. We didn't know enough. We hadn't learned anything except that he wanted a tape that didn't exist. Kit knew what I was doing, and, out of the side of my eye, I saw him move back toward the far end of the catwalk. Neither of us said anything.

"You sonsabitches," Mercer yelled. "What is this?" He stepped onto the catwalk and along it toward me. It brought him almost close enough for me to reach—or for him to reach me. I planted my feet solidly.

"Why do you want a tape, Mercer?" I said. "What could be on a tape that makes you want it so much?"

He wiped sweat off his forehead, and I saw in his eyes the decision to try reason. When someone switches from near rage to reason, it is time to be ready.

"How would I know what's on it, Blade? That's how come I want it, so I can find out what's on it. I'm not going to charge you or Marlow. That was hothead talk. Give the tape to me, and we'll forget you didn't turn it over when you found it."

"No," I said.

He unbuttoned his suit coat with his right hand, and I saw that he carried his short-barreled police special in a belt holster, well back on his right hip and high. I put my hand in my pants pocket. I had the faster gun rig, and I knew I could take him if he reached for his, which I at least half expected him to do. He didn't. My flat refusal had backed him against a wall, and I tried to take advantage of it.

"Did you get yours in a cash bag the first of every month, Mercer? Did you decide you wanted Alexander's share along with yours?" I shot the questions at him. If he made his move, Kit and I had our answer.

"What? What?" If he dissembled, he did it very well. "What the hell are you raving about, Blade?"

"You heard 'im, Mercer," Kit said. "We want answers. We want 'em now."

Import scored with Mercer. He shook his shoulders like a boxer coming up from a surprise knockdown and caught hold of himself. I could see the effort he had to make. He looked at Kit and back at me, and I tried to read his mind as it raced. If he had reason to fear a tape, he had come to kill, and, if he had, he had made too many mistakes. Kit wore his gun. I had my hand on mine. He stood far down on the short end of the odds.

"You think I want the tape because I think it involved me?" he said.

"You out here, ain't you?" Kit said. "Nobody else has come. What other reason you got for bein' here?"

Mercer had a fast mind. "What reason do you have for refusing to give me the tape, Marlow? Maybe you got yours the first of every month."

"No," Kit said. "I could've. I didn't."

"But Alexander did," Mercer said. "All along you knew he did. And you think he got killed because of it." His anger had gone. "If you had a tape, if Blade had found one this morning, you would have played it by now. We wouldn't be standing here playing games. There isn't any tape, is there?"

"No," I said.

"You did a damn good job of faking me out."

"I tried to fake everybody out," I said. I kept my hand on my gun.

"So whoever shot Peters and got the other tapes, the ones Peters found, would scramble out here after one he would think he missed," Mercer said. "And I showed up."

"You showed up," Kit said. He hadn't relaxed any more than I had. He had increased his distance from Mercer and me until he was seventeen or eighteen feet down the catwalk.

Mercer's thought sequences had shifted into high gear. "The pressure you've been putting on Annie and the people up north—you've been trying to force somebody out into the open, somebody who killed Alexander. Did you decide the boys from Kansas City had moved in on you? Did you think they had Alexander killed?"

"We thought it," Kit said.

"Do you now?"

"No," I said. "We've got pretty good reason to be sure they didn't."

"We'll talk more about it, but right now that leaves us Wilson, him and probably his son," Mercer said. "Goddammit, I knew it all along." His black eyes had gotten busy again; they moved restlessly from Kit to me. He hitched at his belt.

"I got to admit you prob'ly right, Mercer," Kit said.

"Hell, yes, I'm right. Maybe now you'll quit dragging ass about getting Wilson."

"Where'd you hear about the tape, the one we don't have?" I asked.

"From Butler," he said. "I guess I owe you an apology, Blade." He put out his right hand for me to shake. Since he wore a right-handed holster, and since he seemed to mean it, I took my hand out of my pocket and reached for his.

He plunged toward me. I thought instantly that I had

151

let him lull me into a mistake he had counted on my making. I moved to the side, out of his path, by instinct. His shoulder hit my arm, not squarely, and he kept on going—down.

His face smashed into the catwalk boards, and he slid, lay without movement, as inert as a half-filled grain sack. He hadn't lifted his hands to ease his fall.

I realized noise had shoved him, first a sudden, meaty thud that sounded like a butcher hitting a beef quarter with the flat of his cleaver, then the ringing, penetrating crack of a high-velocity rifle. I saw in one of those split seconds of frozen, startling visual clarity a small hole in the back of Mercer's suit coat, about four inches below the point where his neck met his shoulders, squarely in the center of the seam. A bullet had hit him in the spine and blasted his brain and his body into death in a microsecond.

I had my gun in my hand and I don't remember throwing it there with the pocket spring. Behind me, Kit's gun crashed deep sound, firing so fast shots blended into roar. Over the roar, I heard again the spiteful crack of the rifle, its report an answering tenor to the pistol's crash. The bullet spun Kit, slammed him into the side of the boat house. He slid on down to the catwalk. His pistol hit the smooth boards, skidded across them, and splashed into the water.

I dived for the planks, holding my head up and searching for a target. I could see nothing. White hot pincers grabbed at my right thigh like a gigantic, punishing metal claw that penetrated front and back, side to side. I heard the rifle for the third time. I waited for another shot, the last one, the one I wouldn't hear. Mercer hadn't heard the one that killed him. I had no place to go, no place to hide, and I couldn't have gotten there if there had been one. I felt no pain now; my leg had numbed quickly.

"Throw away the gun," someone yelled from the top of the hill, off to the left of the path. "Throw it into the water." I did. The splash sounded loud in the silence that had followed the crash and crack of gunfire.

FOURTEEN

Don James, Mercer's partner, stood up from behind a weed screen at the crest of the hill, where he had been lying prone, squeezing off his shots like the expert he probably was. He walked to the path and came down, crossed the planks to the catwalk.

He carried a scoped .270 rifle over his crooked arm, casually, like a man out after woodchucks on an early fall afternoon. The flat trajectory of the .270 makes it a good woodchuck gun, but, with the right ammunition, it's more than enough for a man, too. It had been more than enough for Mercer and Kit and it had left me nearly helpless. James stopped at the edge of the catwalk and motioned to me with the rifle barrel. I did what it directed, pulled myself out of his way with my arms until I had backed against the boat house wall. He sidled past me, never turning the rifle's muzzle away from me.

He grunted satisfaction when he saw the wet, spreading

blotch in the center of Mercer's back. He looked perfunctorily down toward Kit, turned back to face me.

His face looked as calm as if he had just finished shooting a near-perfect score on a rifle range, but his eyes showed that he had enjoyed himself far more with live targets.

I had no appeal to make to him, but I knew that, if I had, his only response would have been amusement. I wouldn't give him that. I had no doubt about his intent: When he left this place, he would leave behind three dead men, and it would be the same to him as if he had left behind three dead fish.

"I could have hit you dead center, too," he said. "I don't miss with a rifle."

"Why didn't you?" I asked. Numbness had begun to leave my leg. From the feel of it, the bullet had punched out bone.

"Time enough," he said. "Where's the tape?"

"What tape?"

He took a step toward me, reached out with the rifle barrel and raked the front sight's edge across my forehead. I must have been half in shock. I moved too late to grab the barrel, and he laughed at me. "I can beat you half way to death, maybe closer," he said. "Or I can shoot you in the other leg, then in one arm and then in the other. I can use my knife on you slow but not easy. There's only you and me, so you may as well tell me now, because you'll tell me before I quit." He would do what he said. I recognized the mind I faced. It wasn't ordinary or normal or even sick, because to get sick, you first have to be well. Evil laughed inside James, pure and untouchable.

"There isn't any tape," I said.

"You got a recorder out from town to play a tape, so there's a tape," he said. "The three I took after I killed

155

Peters didn't have a damn thing on them but a bunch of Ben's legal crap, nothing about me. The one you've got probably has it all."

"All of what, James?"

"I warned Ben once," he said, "and that could have been a mistake. I never make mistakes twice."

"Did you want Ben's share or did he decide to pull out?" I thought and sparred for time. His kind, when they're in command, like to tell how they got there.

"That fool decided to get out when the boys from up north decided to turn the gambling into a big thing. He said he was afraid of the syndicate. I'm not afraid of anything. He said I had to get out with him. Nobody tells me to do anything I don't want to do. With him gone and Marlow gone, I can up my end to fifteen hundred a month, easy."

"So you killed him and raped the girl?" I didn't need his answer, but seconds had become as valuable to me as diamonds—more so. His eyes and his rifle muzzle had never left me, but I needed only a piece of a second if they did.

"She made a fine piece," he said. "A bonus. You should have heard her beg."

"How did you manage about Fred?" I asked.

"That Bessie told me about the tapes he found. I knew he'd be down there alone, so I told Mercer I was going out after cigarettes. Left the motel and was back in twenty minutes. I made it into bed and asleep before you and Marlow called from the jail. You should've seen that snoopy old bastard's face when he knew I was going to shoot him." His blue eyes enjoyed his memory. "You should've seen Ben's face when all along he thought I was in Oklahoma City and there I jumped up in his back yard with a shotgun."

"Mercer wasn't in on any of it?" I asked.

"That law-assed bastard. Look at him now. I saw you and him start to shake hands and I figured you had told him what's on the tape. I parked down the road, walked in and laid down up there and watched you. You and me talked about enough now, Blade. Where is it?"

If I told him it was in the cabin, he'd probably shoot me before he went to look for it. If I didn't tell him there was a tape somewhere, he'd kill me, slowly. If I convinced him there was no tape, he'd kill me anyway; he had to. "The tape's back in town," I said. "I played it out here, then took it back in and turned it over to Butler. He knows what's on it, so you're through, no matter what, James."

He stuck the rifle barrel toward me, stopped its muzzle inches from my eyes. "One finger twitch," he said. "No. Don't move your hands. Don't even blink." He slapped the barrel down across my bloody thigh. Bone grated, and, behind my eyes, I saw raging, concentric red rings. They turned to black and to gray before I could see again. "Maybe you'll learn to quit trying to shit me," he said. "I saw Butler just before I came out here. He said he'd told Haley about the tape and that Haley came out here."

"Butler will know you followed him out here," I said. None of this meant anything, and, if he hit me in the leg again, I wasn't sure I wanted to buy more time.

"That dumb, hick bastard? He thinks I'm on my way to Oklahoma City. I will be after I finish with you and take this rifle back out to Wilson's place. And I'll make damn sure Wilson dies when we find him, before he says a word. I can lay you three on his dead back along with Ben and the girl."

Behind James's legs, I saw Kit move, raise his head. Shock blanked his eyes, but they shifted to James's back and to the rifle butt and comprehension came to them. He looked around for his gun, couldn't find it. Then he reached cautiously, painfully slowly for the little spinning rod that stood propped against the boat house wall. His hand closed on its butt.

"Help me up to the cabin, and I'll show you where the tape is," I told James.

"Just tell me where it is."

"I tell you, and you'll kill me."

"I'll kill you if you don't," he said. "You'll like dying a hell of a lot better if you do."

I agonized with Kit, but I made sure I didn't give him away with my eyes. I heard the sibilant whisper of the rod's tip.

The monofilament line whipped around the side of James's right cheek and across his nose, and, when the glistening little treble-hooked lure slapped his left cheek, Kit struck.

James squealed like a woman and turned his head to the sudden bite and tear of the hooks. His rifle barrel shot up and pointed four feet above my head. My knife slipped sweetly from its sheath, and I had more than enough time.

I've never thrown harder. I hit him three or four inches above his collar bone, well to the left of the center of his stretched, vulnerable throat, and the honed point and edges of the blade made a solid, chunking noise as they drove through his carotid artery and into his spine, leaving less than three inches of my knife's weighted hilt visible.

He died on his feet, blood gushing down over his shirt and tie. He had his finger in the trigger guard and pulled, blew a hole in the tin wall above me, then fell forward toward me, dead when he hit. The rifle clattered and skidded. Blood began to spread beneath his throat, not more than a foot from my leg.

Kit had dropped the rod and was trying to prop himself to a sitting position with his right arm. He couldn't make it. He had been hit high in the left shoulder. I crawled to him, leaving my blood trail behind my right leg.

I propped Kit against the wall, ripped the buttons off his shirt. Blood made it look worse than it was; the bullet hadn't made a lot of hole. A .270 is a neat rifle. I took off my shirt and ripped it, got a compress behind his shoulder and another on the entry hole. He leaned against the wall to hold the one on his back in place, held the one in front with his right hand.

"Take care of yourself," he said.

"It's not bad enough to worry about," I said. A lie. It worried me, but I hadn't lost enough blood to count seriously, probably wouldn't. "A hell of a good cast."

"You done fine with the gaff," he said.

Neither of us had anything more to say. We sat for a minute, looking at each other.

"I'll tell you the truth," he said. "I doubt I can git up that hill."

"I can make it," I said.

"I got two legs. You ain't got but one left," he said. "I'll wait a minute or so and then I'll try it."

I tried to get to my feet, got my left one under me, lurched with sudden dizziness, and put weight on my right one, and fell. The pain fired off rockets in my head. I lay there a minute before I sat back up.

"It's busted, ain't it?" Kit said.

"Feels that way."

"My turn." He got as far as his knees before his head bowed; "Shooo," he said, and fainted, falling onto his face. The compress I had put behind his shoulder had crusted to his wound and stuck there.

Later I started to crawl on two hands and one knee. I made it down the catwalk and across the planks that reached from dock to shore, started up the steep gravel path. All I could think of was that I'd probably never get up the steps to the sun deck.

I didn't hear Swimmer come down the path to me. I was concentrating too hard on staying conscious and on trying to gain another foot or two.

"Whoa," Swimmer said. "You made it far enough on your own. I'll take over from here on in."

"Kit's down on the dock," I said. Darkness had come, and the boat house bulked as shadow below me. "He's worse. You'd better get to him."

"You all right for me to leave you?" He kneeled beside me.

"I'm all right."

He came back up the path carrying Kit in his arms as easily as I would carry a child. "He's breathin'," he said. "Them other two down there ain't."

"Take him on up to the house," I said.

"I'll be back for you."

"Call an ambulance first." I felt light-headed and weak, a little ashamed I hadn't made it all the way up the path, relieved that I wouldn't have to try the steps up to the cabin. They had loomed higher than Everest.

Swimmer came back, lifted me without straining, and carried me to the cabin. The steps didn't bother him.

He had put Kit on one of the couches. Kit had some color, but he was still unconscious. He rolled his head.

My leg no longer bled, and Swimmer lowered me into one of the big chairs in front of the fireplace. "Be ten, fifteen minutes 'fore they git here," he said. "I figger it's better'n loadin' you into my pickup."

"You hear what the turtle told the honorary Cherokee?" I said.

"No."

"He said he could damn well use a drink."

"Man has got to listen to the turtle," he said. He went to the bar and brought back a half glass of Daniel's. "Doctor'd tell you not to drink that. Bad in your condition."

I drank about half of it, leaned back and waited for the warmth. It came quickly. My head spun a little, so I took the other half.

"Was it both of 'em?" Swimmer asked.

"Just James."

"He did all the shootin'?"

"All of it," I said. "Ben and the girl and Fred. You believe in doctors, what they say about good whisky?"

"Not all the time."

"I will take about two fingers more."

I didn't have a comfortable ambulance ride back to Catherton, but I didn't care.

FIFTEEN

In the middle of the afternoon of the second day, a nurse wheeled Kit into my hospital room. I had been demanding that they take me in to see him, but they had insisted the cast on my leg made that impossible. He wore a body cast that held his left arm in a horizontal position.

"You fixin' to fly?" I asked.

"About as soon as you fixin' to walk," he said. "How you feel?"

"Crippled."

"They told me your leg's busted."

"How about you?"

"I will be stove up for awhile," he said.

"I'll be out in two weeks," I said.

"Then I'll be out in one. First liar don't have a chance. Swimmer come by yestiddy?"

"I saw him," I said. "He wanted me to get up and go help him stack another bar."

"Hirsh has disappeared," he said. "Damn good riddance.

162

He figgered I'd slap charges on 'im for that dynamite. You see Ma?"

"She is going to bring me a three-pound sirloin for dinner." Ma had cried the day before when she came in to see me, had thanked me through tears that I knew were a true compliment.

"She better bring two," he said. "You give Billy Joe your statement?"

"He got it," I said.

"Mine, too. On a damn tape recorder. I will be just as happy if'n I don't have to fool with any more recorders."

"I don't intend to find any more tapes."

"It worked, Jud."

"Damn near too well," I said. "You will have to teach me how to cast."

"You can learn me to th'ow a knife."

"I asked Swimmer to make sure I get it back, my gun, too."

"You'll git 'em," he said. "I wouldn't want you to be without 'em."

"Did you suspect James, Kit?"

"No. I should've. He was up here too much 'fore Ben got killed. Did you?"

For reason of pride, I wish I could have said I had. "No."

"Too bad about Mercer. I didn't like 'im much, but he was a good lawman."

"Nearly all of them are good, Kit." I believe this: You run into a James far less frequently than you have any hope or real right to expect.

Swimmer filled the door to the hospital room. "See-oh," he said. "Looks like what used to be left of a wagon train after my noble red ancestors got through with the invadin' white eyes."

"You bring what I told you to?" Kit asked.

"You tryin' to git me arrested," Swimmer said. He reached behind him and shut the door, put his hand up under the front of his loose, tent-sized sport shirt, and pulled out an unlabeled pint bottle. "But us redskins is still sneaky; we got to be to git by them nurses." He crossed the room and handed me the bottle.

I uncapped it, careful not to inhale, because I had learned the secret: Moonshine tastes fine as long as you don't smell it first. I took a highly satisfactory taste.

"Save me some, dammit," Kit said. I gave Swimmer the bottle, and he handed it to Kit, who took his taste, about six swallows. "You bring any extra, blanket butt?"

"One for him and one for you," Swimmer said. He pulled out two more pint bottles from under his shirt, gave one to me and one to Kit. I put mine in the drawer of the bedside table, and Kit tucked his in under the blanket that covered him from the waist down. Swimmer put the first bottle, almost empty, back under his shirt.

"You could hide a barrel of beer under there," Kit said.

"Have. Often," Swimmer said. "Anything else I can do for you invalids?"

"Not 'till tomorry," Kit said. "You told Tug he could come on out?"

"Last night."

"Don't figger you had any trouble findin' 'im," Kit said.

"Him and Caleb was back up past Turkey Rock," Swimmer said.

"Hell, I knew that," Kit said. "Prob'ly on that north fork of Chicken Creek. Tell Tug I'll be out to see 'im soon's I can."

"I'll tell 'im," Swimmer said.

The door opened and Ma came in. She wore a dark-blue silk dress with a tiny white figure in it and a blue straw hat. She carried a big, blue straw purse.

"Squaw does not belong with wounded warriors," Swimmer said.

"This ain't your teepee, heathen," she said. She grinned at him, and he took her hand. I saw they were friends.

"Let's you and me go stomp dancin' tonight," he said. "My competition is outta the way."

"Pick me up about eight," she said. She took her hand back from Swimmer and came to me, felt my forehead, put her purse down and straightened my pillow. I heard the purse clink when it touched the floor.

"He is too young for you, old woman," Kit said.

"We've got an understanding," I said.

Ma smiled at me, leaned over to straighten my top sheet. She sniffed. She went to Kit and leaned down into his face. "Shooo," she said. "Come to see sick folks and find a bunch of drunks. Where's it hid?"

"Nosy squaw," Swimmer said. "Needs her nose notched."

"And you brung it in," she said. "Pull up that shirt."

"Never," Swimmer said.

I leaned over the side of my bed and picked up her purse, heard it gurgle. I reached in and pulled out a pint of Jack Daniel's.

"Squaw bootlegger," Swimmer said.

"You under arrest," Kit said.

"Put that away before a nurse comes in," Ma said. "I only brought it because I didn't want you drinkin' that squirrel whisky these two drink."

I put the bottle in the table drawer with the other one.

"I got to go before the warden comes in and holds a shakedown," Swimmer said. "I will see you all later." He left. The room seemed less like a crowded closet.

Ma stayed about ten minutes. "I will be back at supper time with that steak, Jud," she said.

"I have been beat out by a Yankee," Kit said.

She put her hand on his shoulder and smiled down at

him. "You stay sober enough to eat yours," she said. She straightened my sheet, which didn't need it, a last time, picked up her bag and left.

"Good to have friends," Kit said.

"Real good." He and I knew we both thought the same thing: There is no friendship as tight as the one formed when two men look at death together and then live to look at life.

"You never got to try out my boat," Kit said. "We git outta this damn place, and I will take you fishin'. Big-mouth hit good on chubs the first part of October."

"Sounds good," I said.

"Then you'll be walkin' all right along about the time quail season starts. I got me a fine-workin' pair of setters."

"I've never hunted over a dog," I said.

"Nine-tenths of quail huntin' is watchin' a good dog work. Look, you will be awhile mendin' after they let us outta here. You welcome to use that cabin as long as you want, Jud. I'd admire for you to."

"How would you feel about selling half of that cabin?"

He looked at me quickly. "I'd have to have at least four dollars from you," he said. "Wait a minute. You the kind to bring women in?"

"Frequently," I said.

"I will cut it to three dollars. You serious, ain't you?"

"I'm serious," I said.

"Let's have us a drink on it."

"Fine." I waited on him.

He grinned. "You got two bottles," he said. "I am gonna need mine later on."